Dedicated to:
Laurence James
A true friend indeed, especially when
things get 'spooky'

DEATH IN THE CANYON

DEATH IN THE CANYON

by

Jim A. Nelson

Dales Large Print Books
Long Preston, North Yorkshire,
BD23 4ND, England.

British Library Cataloguing in Publication Data.

Nelson, Jim A.
    Death in the canyon.

    A catalogue record of this book is
    available from the British Library

    ISBN   978-1-84262-792-1 pbk

First published in Great Britain in 1997 by Robert Hale Limited

Cover illustration © Michael Thomas

Published in Large Print 2011 by arrangement with
Mike Stotter

Dales Large Print is an imprint of Library Magna Books Ltd.

Printed and bound in Great Britain by
T.J. (International) Ltd., Cornwall, PL28 8RW

ONE

Billy Joe Brecker stepped down on to the porch of his ranch house and stopped to take in a deep breath. The way he dressed reminded me of a tailor's dummy I'd once seen in Miles City rather than a Montanan ranchman.

You could see the nervousness showing in the way his big brown eyes kept blinking and the way he ran his fingers through his dark, straight hair. For a ranchman who spent the better part of the day out in the merciless sun his face was curiously pale and unblemished by time or weather. His skin was pulled tight like chicken skin across his facial bones. From bunkhouse talk I'd learned that he'd only been in this part of the country for a half-year.

Big Tony Brecker – his father – wanted his

son to learn about life first hand and not from a world of books in a city that was hundreds of miles away from 'real life'; so he sent him out West. Billy Joe Brecker had inherited the Leaning B when his uncle had died a short while ago after he drowned in a swimming accident in the Yellowstone River. The kid was certainly learning about 'real life' the hard way.

He wiped the back of his hand over his lips, and looked over at me. He put on his hat, adjusted the setting, and angled over to the corral. Over on my right some of the ranch hands were lined up outside of the bunkhouse hoping that their boss would have a change of heart and let them ride along. Although I was a hired hand, I was not a thirty-and-found man. I had been bunking down with them for the last two weeks and one or two of the cowboys confided in me that they would relish the opportunity to square up to the DR rannies. The DR was a local outfit that bordered the Leaning B whose boss seemed to relish bullying Brecker around.

Brecker's refusal to let the men ride into town with us upset Jake Latchford, the top hand. Earlier on I had pointed out that he was being paid to look after the cattle and I was being paid to look after the man. Latchford realised that there was no point in arguing any further.

I sat astride a long-legged sorrel I called Tag. He was named after my first boss, Don Tag, being that they were of the same disposition. Without a word I handed Brecker the reins to his saddled grey. He nodded his thanks, settled himself on leather and looked me squarely in the eyes. 'Can I depend on you, Will?' he asked a little uneasily.

'You've paid me, haven't you?' I answered, pushing back my shoulders to sit taller in the saddle, a little hurt by his question. A cold wind was blowing down the canyon from over the north end of the Powder River Ridge, so I pulled up the collar of my sheepskin jacket to shield my neck. Even though spring was just around the corner, winter wasn't going to give up without a fight.

Obviously Brecker wasn't sure about my answer and pressed me some more. 'I know I've paid you, Calhoun, but you've been with me for a couple o' weeks now, and well … y'know what I'm trying to say.'

'I know,' I said, trying to ignore the fact that he had switched to calling me by my surname, and looked the rancher in the eye. 'Don't go forgetting that I was right there in the general store when you made your threat to Raley. I knew that you needed my help after that.'

The answer seemed to satisfy Brecker because he smiled for the first time that day. He jerked the grey's head towards the town trail that angled away north out of the canyon, and kicked the horse into a walk, heading out of his yard. He looked over his shoulder to see if I was following. He needn't have troubled himself – I was.

The start of our journey was made in silence and this gave me the chance to remind myself of how I came to work for Billy Joe Brecker and the Leaning B. I'd been previously working as a shotgun rider for a mine over Helena way and was being paid to take a shipment to Miles City along with two other guards. We were three-quarters of the way there when some bandits tried to take it away from us. Naturally we put up a good fight, but Dean Roberts was killed and Carlos was wounded a couple of times. We managed to hold off the bandits until some citizens saw fit to intervene and we got the better of the road agents.

I got both the gold and Carlos safely to Miles City, then promptly got paid off without further thanks. To say I felt low would be an understatement and I went on a three-day drunk. When I finally came to my senses I was broke again but thankful that I hadn't sunk so low as to sell my saddle. Miles City was way too rich for my blood, so I headed south.

I arrived in Huntings with my last dollar in my pocket and headed for the general store. That's when I met up with Brecker who was having a shouting match with Dave Raley, the owner of the DR outfit. The boy was threatening the bigger man with all kinds of ills if he didn't have his cattle returned. Raley just laughed him off and said that he'd take him on any time, then went out of the store.

Brecker turned and began to bewail his luck to Christine Dyer, the storeowner, and for some reason I butted in and offered my services. Naturally he was sceptical at first but I soon won him around and started my job as his bodyguard right there and then. The woman didn't like it, you could see that from the look she gave me when we were leaving the store. Brecker was obviously too inexperienced in this type of rough-necked cattle business to handle the trouble himself. My offer of help must have been like manna from Heaven.

Pulling alongside I looked over at my boss and his face betrayed every thought crossing his mind. He used his shirt-sleeve to mop at his sweating face and the constant blinking told me that he was thinking about the up-coming confrontation with Dave Raley at the stockyard to the east of town.

The morning sun was burning brightly as we left the ranch behind us and rode at an easy pace that allowed us to reach town by late morning. We entered Huntings by the way of the arrow-straight Main Street. Brecker slowed his grey so that we rode alongside each other. It seemed that word had got out about the up-coming set-to and people were lining the sidewalk to watch the spectacle. Brecker was uneasy under such scrutiny but much of life was learned this way and this was a scene I had been in many a time so wasn't fazed by it all.

As we rode level to the widow Dyer's store, the diminutive but beautifully proportioned figure of Christine Dyer stood in the doorway. She waved a hand to Brecker and he smiled at her in return.

I said, 'Keep your mind on Raley, Billy Joe.'

Brecker's smile faltered and he looked down Main towards the stockyard. To tell you the truth it wasn't a stockyard in the truest sense. The Parsons Holding Company, a private yard with big ambitions, was financed by Dave Parsons and his brothers, Mark and Jeremiah. It was nothing like the Union Stockyards in Chicago, but given time it might grow that way. It already covered four acres and you could see more work going on away to the north. There were all the trappings of a regular stockyard though; a small community of cattlemen and their cowboys were camped around it; stock detectives had their offices there; railroad men; cattle buyers and reporters of stock news were also there. On this day it seemed like the world and his wife were there, waiting.

We got to Main and First where Dave Raley with fifteen of his men were waiting for us. Brecker swallowed nervously. No doubt the tension was building up inside of him, and even I hadn't expected this kind of turn out.

'Is that the marshal, there?' Brecker said hopefully.

I looked over towards the barber's shop, and Town Marshal John Evans was sitting in a rocker on the porch, rolling himself a smoke.

'Yeah, he's there, all right,' I whispered. 'Just to make sure there's no gunplay.'

Brecker frowned, then said, 'His being there means that he's not going to let Raley stop me getting my cattle, Calhoun.'

I shrugged. 'He might be the town marshal but he ain't going to interfere with a private argument. Not unless one of you hauls iron. Don't depend on John backing up your play, he'll remain independent so long as...'

'I know!' Brecker interrupted. 'But he's a good friend.'

'Mine too, but a lawman first. He's a good sort of individual who likes to draw his monthly pay and doesn't take to being troubled. I remember down in El Paso some while back, John was sheriff and I got into a shooting match with some feller who turned out to be mighty popular with the townsfolk. John Evans ran me out of town. I guess if he hadn't, they might have had themselves a necktie party with me as their guest of honour. Doing it that way, we remained friends. So think about his responsibility first, Billy Joe.'

Brecker nodded slowly. His face was ashen and he licked at his dry lips. We rode our horses over to the hitching rail outside the gunsmith's and the rancher dismounted. I noticed that Brecker was slow in getting down on the ground and tying up the grey, double-checking the knot and fiddling with the cinch. I was impatient to get things done, and said, 'C'mon, Billy Joe, time to be going.'

The one thing I didn't do was to take my eyes off Raley's men. Dismounting I slipped off the hammer thong on the blindside of most people. One of the things I've learned was not to scare anyone into using their gun but I had to be ready.

Brecker nodded and began to walk to-wards Parsons's yard. Walking slowly with me at his side seemed to give him a boost of confidence that he needed so badly. He fairly strutted down the street keeping his eyes on Dave Raley as the man stepped away from his men. Raley was round-faced, large in the middle and heavily muscled arms poked out from his rolled-up sleeves. He planted his thick legs wide waiting for us to approach. He was big, but no taller than me.

His men formed a straggly line behind him. I instantly recognised the ramrod, Brian Haydon, and his son, Russ. Two other faces that were familiar were the cadaverous Brian Gillman and a short, bow-legged bronc-buster named Dave Percy. I'd seen these two hardcases at work one time in town and they were mean. The others I didn't know but figured wouldn't count as a threat if push came to shove.

Town Marshal John Evans struck a match and lit up. He fixed his eyes on Billy Joe Brecker and gave a slight nod, then turned his attention to Dave Raley. The big man gave him a contemptuous smile and said,

'Figgered you'd be here, John.'

Evans stayed silent and gave him a dead-eyed look in return.

We walked up to Raley until we were no more than ten feet apart, then the young rancher stopped. I wanted to close the gap a little more, to put the advantage our way but settled on moving slightly to one side. I waited with thumbs tucked into my waistband. Raley kept an eye on me, knowing where the real threat was coming from, but spoke to Brecker.

'Brecker, I told you more 'n a week ago, you're not taking them cattle out of town,' he announced.

Brecker's voice was low but shaky. 'I'm taking them, Raley, and there ain't a thing you can do to stop me.'

'Oh there's not, is there?'

Brecker gained a little confidence and ventured an insult. 'You ain't that big in the country, Raley. I mean to move *my* cattle right now!'

Dave Raley raised an eyebrow in mock

amusement and turned his head slowly towards the marshal. 'Did you hear that, Marshal?'

'Uh-huh.'

Raley turned back to the Leaning B owner. 'Them cattle stay where they are. I'm not the only rancher 'round here that doesn't want them diseased-ridden critters let loose on the range. You, nor anybody else is going to do that.' He openly challenged Brecker to retaliate by taking one step closer and jabbing his stubby forefinger at Brecker. 'You mouthed off in front of me and witnesses that you were going to move them by force. Now either play your hand or back off!'

Brecker swallowed hard and returned Raley's hot gaze. 'There ain't a damn' thing wrong with them cattle, Dave, and you know it! They're a new breed that's fit for the range, and given time will sire better, fatter cattle that will increase everyone's profits. You're just pissed that I beat you to the deal – this time round.'

Raley's nostrils flared with anger and he moved back, his right hand sweeping close to his holstered weapon.

'For a little runt, you sure got a big mouth. You're going to have to come past me to get at 'em, Brecker.'

I figured that if Raley went for his gun things would get out of hand, I had to stop it. 'Move away,' I said to my boss.

'Keep out of this, *boy*,' Raley said without taking his eyes off Brecker. 'Well?'

Brecker took a deep breath and lunged at Raley, his arm cocked back for a haymaker. The man was ready for him and simply stepping aside drove out a straight right hander. His massive fist caught Brecker on the chin and he was sent sprawling to the ground, kicking up a cloud of dust as he hit the dirt. Brian Haydon let out a hearty laugh as the rancher went down, he knew his boss had the beating of the smaller man. I could see that he was keeping me in his vision. That was good, I had him worried.

Raley's face was split by an evil smile as he

kicked at Brecker's stomach just as the youngster had pushed himself on to all fours. Brecker let out a yelp of pain and fell back to the ground. I figured it was time for me to intervene and save the boss from a serious beating. I began to lunge for Raley, but even before I had gotten anywhere near him to throw my punch, I heard the *click-clack* of a gun being cocked close to my ear, and I slowly, carefully, turned around.

'Don't interfere, Calhoun,' Evans ordered. His Colt was pointed in my face in a steady grip. Evans moved his second gun to cover the other men, especially Brian Haydon who had his hand on the grips of his Colt. Evans shook his head slowly as a warning for not to do anything, and Haydon's hand fell away. 'This is between Raley and Brecker, so I don't want *anyone* butting in. I see anyone else going for their iron I'll plug 'em. Understand?'

I knew that Evans was right. If I did step in, then Haydon would jump me, and that meant the marshal would have to commit himself to one side or another. And without doubt, all hell would break loose in a free for all, and someone would end up dead. All I could do was simply stand there with Evans's gun covering me, and give Raley a cold stare I usually saved for my worst enemies. Raley had been elevated to that rank now. The big man slowly turned his gaze away and watched Brecker rise painfully to his feet.

At that moment I knew that it was over, right there and then. The young rancher was beaten, the look of utter dejection, mixed with fear was on his face as plain as day. He had always been afraid of Raley but he had told everyone that he was going to take his cattle away from Raley whether he liked it or not. It was a moment of pure madness that had brought Brecker to his knees and when he spoke, everything was confirmed.

'This ain't fair, Raley!' he all but sobbed. 'They're my cattle, not yourn or anyone else's. I've got legal rights to 'em.'

Raley's top lip curled in contempt. 'An' I got a legal piece of paper saying they're all infected with cattle tick, an' that means they stay put until the vet deals with 'em, an' gives 'em the OK.'

Brecker turned to Evans for help. 'You can't let him do this, John.'

Evans shifted uneasily under Brecker's pleading eyes. 'I'm sorry, Billy Joe, but as long as the vet says them beeves are infected, they stay where they are.'

It looked like those special cattle were staying put. Dave Raley unknotted his large fists and smiled triumphantly at Brecker.

He knew that he had won the fight and broken Brecker in the same process. He couldn't hide the pleasure in his voice when he said, 'Next time I'll kill you.'

John Evans slipped home his pistols saying, 'I'll have no talk of killing, Raley, or you'll be tangling with me, understand?'

Raley glared at the marshal, then turned to his men signalling with a jerk of his chin that everything was over. He brushed past Brecker as he swaggered back towards the line of DR ponies, his men following him. As

Brian Haydon drew alongside me he stopped and sneered in my face. 'You ain't nothing but a coontail rattler, mister!' he said.

I wasn't going to be goaded into a fight by some no-good badass, so I remained silent. Haydon spat on the ground arrogantly and joined the others. I kept an eye on him for a moment or two, then turned back to my boss as he swayed unsteadily on his feet dusting himself off. Brecker retrieved his battered hat and put it back on his head. He couldn't help wincing with pain as he raised his arm.

He looked at me and said, 'You think it's over, Will?'

'At least you tried where others have failed,' came my slow reply. 'Trouble is, Raley and others like him have had it their way for so long. They just ain't going to roll over and let someone else take over the range.'

'But I don't want all the range, you know that. Them cattle are the next generation to feed the country and make everyone a heap of money at the same time. I'm not going to stop DR cattle or anyone else's roaming on to our land. If those bulls sire anyone else's cows then that's fine; they can keep the calves and bring up a different, hardier breed.' He shook his head slowly in dismay.

'They're not diseased and he knows it.'

'And don't forget he's got a few people in his pocket,' I had to remind him.

'I hope you're not including me in that statement, Will,' Town Marshal Evans said, approaching us.

'You know I don't, John,' I answered easily. I knew that he wouldn't be insulted by what I had said because we both knew that he wasn't included in my comment. 'But you know that Raley and others have a handful of important people on their payroll.'

'Yeh, and there ain't a damned thing I can do about it,' Evans rasped. 'I can't get one bit of evidence that would stick against nary a one of them. And, believe me, I've tried my damnedest. Who cares? In six months' time they'll elect another town marshal and I'll be moving on. It'll be someone else's problem then.'

Brecker said, 'That's OK by me, John. I trust you.'

'Thanks, Billy Joe. But remember I'm still the law around here and I expect you to obey my rules.'

Brecker nodded and cast his eyes downwards.

'I don't know about you two, but I need a beer,' I suggested to break the uneasy silence. 'Join me?'

'You go ahead,' replied Brecker. 'I think I'll go see Chris.'

'I've got other business to tend to, thanks all the same,' Evans excused himself and headed toward his office on Main. I suppose he knew full well that the incident wasn't going to be just an isolated case. Both Brecker and myself walked over to the hitching rail, and mounted up. The rancher turned to me and said, 'You never gave me a straight answer, Will. Do you think I'm a coward?'

There was no need for me to lie to the boy. 'Heck no. You made a mistake by telling everyone what you were going to do is all.'

Brecker frowned and said, 'What's the wrong in that?'

'Well I've learned that there are two ways for a person to be. There's the man who's just a lot of wind and piss who huffs and threatens, but nothing comes of it. Then there's the other who's quiet and lets his actions talk for him.'

'You count yourself as the latter?'

'I've survived these twenty-five years, and I'm planning on staying around for a few more besides. I can recall a time in Texas at a place named Eagle Pass, it's well known for being a bad place. There was this loud-mouthed sonofa who picked on this little fella who was standing at the bar enjoying a refreshing cup of *mezcal*. He wasn't inter-fering with anyone – just having a drink to cut the dust from his throat. The rowdy had his pistol out and was waving it around like a goddamn flag on the fourth of July telling the little guy what he was going to do an' all. The little fella calmly put down his cup, and listened to the other's ranting and raving, but at the same time drew out his own pistol and shot the rowdy in the mouth. Blew the back of his head clean off. Then went back to his drink.'

It was clear that Brecker had learned a hard lesson from his fight with Dave Raley, and I hoped that he wouldn't be taken by surprise like that again. The youngster's eye was already puffed-up and half-closed; his jaw was decorated with a purple and black bruise. As we rode on the tension seemed to be draining out of him.

'I reckon you won't be needing me now,' I said, breaking the short silence between us.

'On the contrary, Will. I'd like for you to stay on for a while.'

I smiled at Brecker's way of speaking. You could tell his eastern education was always there, and said, 'That's what I was afraid you was going to say.'

'Damnit, Will! I ain't finished with Raley, not by a long stretch.' Anger reddened Brecker's face. 'I'm not firing you. Stay, please.'

I almost winced at Brecker's girlish whining but nodded.

'Sure. I'll stay and help you get your cattle back.'

Brecker's spirits were lifted at this and he slapped me hard on the shoulder. 'Good man. Raley'll see that he can't go round stomping on people. We'll show him.'

The bravado was back in Brecker's voice and I was pleased that the young rancher had found a rock to cling to in the storm. I knew he had to stop thinking of what others thought about him and begin to develop his own character. I've met his like all over the country and knew that if he went up against the world-wise Raley, he'd be wiped out. I suppose there was something in Brecker I could recognise. I don't know exactly what, but it struck a chord within me and maybe that was the reason why I was so willing to help him.

We drew up to Dyer's Store and Brecker hauled in. He touched the brim of his hat and dismounted. As he went through the doorway he removed his hat and hand-slicked down his hair. That was the kind of enchantment Christine Dyer had on Brecker. She was only a couple of years older than the boy. From what I had learned from local bar-talk she'd been widowed for about a year. Her husband had been killed in an accident as he was loading a wagon. It had been a stupid accident: a rope gave way and a barrel fell on top of him breaking his neck. Since then there had been a few admirers but when Brecker showed up he seemed to become her favourite, and only recently there had been some talk of marriage.

To give her credit, Christine cut a great figure and she dressed very simply with every outfit showing off her figure to the best advantage. Of the times that I'd been in town I had never seen her messed up; her hair was always in place, her clothes clean and she had a ready smile on her rounded face. Today was no exception; she wore a plain cotton dress edged with white lace over which was a stiff white apron. For such a young woman she looked very matronly and I wondered if it was that which appealed to young Brecker.

In the store window there was a gaily painted handbill that had the words:

THE CIRCUS IS COMING SOON

And below that there was a painting of a tiger, teeth bared, leaping through a hoop of fire. I'd never seen a circus in all my life and hoped that I was around these parts long enough to get to see this one. I wheeled Tag around and headed for the Bull Tavern over on Third Avenue.

TWO

By the time the batwings had closed behind me and I saw Raley and his men drinking at the bar it was too late for me to turn around. I crossed the big room and walked past them. The place was full of cowboys talking about the Raley/Brecker set-to over their beers. As I approached the bar it felt like every eye was turned towards me and a hush fell over the place.

The Bull Tavern was typical of any cowtown drinking place: long and narrow; low-ceilinged with a bar running down its length on the right; at the far end were a couple of billiard tables (both in use) and large kerosene lamps hung from the ceiling beams giving out a smoky light. A few round tables took up the rest of the floor space, and were filled by the lunchtime trade of card players and drinkers.

I made my way down the bar to where the billiard tables were, all the while keeping watch on the DR's rannies in the mirror that hung on the wall behind the bar. They, in turn, watched me. I ordered a beer, paid for it and drained half in one toss. I rested up against the bar, keeping my back covered to make sure that no one could creep up on me. Looking across to Raley, the man stared back with an insolent gaze. Brian Gillman and Dave Percy were open-mouthed with amazement that I should have chosen this saloon to walk into. I was amazed myself but a cold stare quietened them.

I brought out my pipe and tobacco, and began to fill the bowl. I became aware that Raley and some of his crew were creeping down the bar towards me. Those drinkers that were between me and the advancing ranchmen quickly moved out of the way, fearful of the consequence of being near two volatile factions.

I continued to ignore them until I had

struck a match and was lowering it to the pipe bowl when it was blown out. I looked around into the leering face of Dave Raley. Behind him stood Gillman, Percy and off to the right the expectant face of Brian Haydon. They were crowding me in, like they were isolating a steer for branding. Well, I wasn't prepared to be branded, not by these men anyhows.

I said, 'You got a problem, Raley?'

'I got a thing about pipe smoke, Calhoun.'

I ignored him and brought out another match but Raley gripped my forearm in a steel-trap grip and hissed, 'You and Brecker are through in these parts, you know it. I want you out of that canyon by the end of the week.'

'That a threat you're making, mister?' I asked.

Raley smiled evilly. 'Not a threat: a promise.'

Haydon laughed and edged a little closer. Raley turned his face away and joined his laughter but it was cut off by my hard fist smashing into his mouth. It sent the rancher falling backwards, arms windmilling and he crashed down on a table. Glasses, cards, coins and three drinkers went with him to the floor.

The sudden outburst of violence brought everyone's attention our way. And just for a split second the DR rannies stayed immobile. The older Haydon was the first to move; rushing over to get his bleeding boss back on to his feet. The others were frozen to the spot, unsure of what to do. Raley shook his head as he slowly got to his feet. There was blood dribbling down from his nose and his top lip was split; already beginning to puff up. That added fuel to his rage and he closed his hands into two massive fists and lurched towards me.

It's true what they say about big men, that they don't always make the best fighters. He was slow and cumbersome in his first attack. I watched the man come on; his shoulders bunching up readying to strike out. The rancher's punch was telegraphed so much that I might have expected it to arrive by Western Union. I simply weaved to the right and at the same time brought up a right in a jaw-smashing upper-cut. It was quickly followed by a straight left jab into Raley's right eye.

The man went down again with blood seeping from a wide gash above his eye, right on the bone. He fell to his knees and I gave him some of his own medicine, lashing out with a boot, and caught him in the brisket. He half turned; arms outstretched, and fell face first on the sawdust covered floor.

Then all hell broke loose. DR rannies came on to me from every which way and there were fists and boots flying everywhere. I got in some good punches before I went down with a numbing blow to the back of my head. A red mist closed down my vision as more fists, knees and boots went to work on my unprotected body.

I rolled across the floor away from more blows. A length of wood dug into my side and I grabbed desperately for it. I managed to get to my knees and brought up the billiard cue around in a savage arc, heaving it with all my strength. There was a dull *thwack* – someone shouted, then the line broke as men stumbled to get out of the way.

Senses reeling, body bruised and aching, and thankful that I remained on my feet, I fought against the rising nausea and swung the cue up above my shoulder. I stood there, wide-legged, face puffing and feeling blood streaking down my cheeks. I was ready to smash the cue into the first individual who was fool enough to rush in. I must have been a sight to behold because none of them did.

Raley and his men stood in a gasping line, their fists clenched and eyes slitted as they faced me apprehensively.

'C'mon!' I panted, and hefted the cue higher. 'Who's gonna be the first to have his head stoved in?'

'Crowd him!' Dave Raley ordered but the words slurred because of his busted mouth.

'Like hell!' said Dave Percy.

'He'll brain us with that thing,' Brian Haydon puffed.

Raley's lips curled and his hand dropped to his gun but as he did the batwings slammed back violently and John Evans, guns in hands, came storming in.

'Get the hell back,' he roared, waving the revolvers dangerously at Raley and his men. He kept coming down the room, through the crowd of spectators, his eyes locked on Raley. When Raley's men showed no sign of moving, the town marshal snapped, 'Move 'em, Raley, or by God you'll have your leg shot from under you.'

Evans cocked the .45s to emphasise that he meant business. Raley's eyes blazed with hate at the lawman momentarily before he stepped away from me. His men followed suit, moving back several paces until Evans seemed satisfied. Thankful for the lawman's timely intervention I dropped the billiard cue with a clatter, and sagged back against a table, my legs feeling wobbly under me.

John Evans raked his eyes over the group

of cattlemen and there was something akin to pleasure sparkling in his eyes when he saw Raley's and Haydon's battered faces.

'Guess it's too late to tell you Calhoun's handy with his fists.' He could hardly keep the smile off his face as he told them about me. 'I've seen him being hit three ways from Sunday by better men than you, and still come back to lick 'em.'

Raley scowled and dabbed at his split eyebrow with his kerchief. 'Seems you're a friend of this drifter, Marshal.'

'I am,' Evans admitted readily. 'I've known Calhoun for a few years now. But friend or not, I'll step in and stop any pack of coyotes from ganging up agin a lone man.'

He turned to ask if I was OK. I was mopping blood from my face with a shirt sleeve, nodded, then said, 'You knew this was coming, didn't you?' It wasn't a question it was a statement.

Evans shrugged. 'Yeh, but I didn't know it would be this quick in coming around. All right, Raley, you've had your fun. You and your men clear out of here. Now!'

Raley ignored the marshal and said to me, 'Remember what I said, Calhoun. You're through in these parts. Ride on.'

I spat out some blood. 'Go to hell,' I replied slowly and clearly, watching the anger flare in Raley's eyes. Out of spite I added, 'I wouldn't leave now, Raley, not if you paid me a thousand dollars.'

He appeared in two minds whether to reply or not, but turned abruptly around, pushed his men roughly out of his way and went out of the door. Me, Evans and the rest of the saloon's customers watched the rannies shuffle along in their boss's wake.

The town marshal sighed heavily, and put away his guns. He was one of a handful of men I knew who was dangerous with a brace of guns.

'That's twice in less than an hour I've hauled iron for you,' he said. 'It's only going to be a matter of time until I get to use these.'

'Sorry about that, John.'

'I see you still got that mean streak running

through you, Will. Raley's giving you good warning to leave town. He's a mean son-ofagun but you're going to stay come hell or high water, aint you? Now, who d'you think I'm going to back when the time comes, tell me that?'

I shrugged. 'You're a law enforcer, John. You know what you've got to do, so don't ask me. I'm not clearing out whilst I'm still working for Brecker.'

Evans rubbed a hand over his face. 'Yeh, I known you since you were busting heads as a youngster. Even if you wanted to move you wouldn't just to give Raley merry hell. Well, now we've got that settled you had better come with me.'

'Where? You ain't arresting me, are you?'

'No, but that's not a bad idea. I'm taking you to the doc's. You haven't seen the state of your face, have you? There's a slit that'll probably need sewing up, but she'll be able to tell you better than me.'

'She?'

'Ah, ah! I thought that might get you

interested,' Evans grinned. 'Doc Bay's been here a couple of years. She's good, so good that I even trust her.'

'No, I can handle it.'

'For once in your life, do as I tell you.' He took me by the arm and led me out of the wrecked saloon, throwing over his shoulder to the owner that the DR would pick up the bill for any damages. He all but dragged me down the street to where Doctor Bay had her practice in the building next door to his own office.

Evans pushed open the door without knocking and tugged me inside. The room was large and well lit by three Rochester lamps burning in different parts of the room. There was a smell to the place that I couldn't put my finger on right off. Then it came to me – the smell of the soapberry tree fruit that a Mexican laundry in Laredo used in its wash. I was amazed that someone this far north would have ever heard of it but then again a doctor's knowledge is gathered from many sources, so who's to say she didn't know about that tree?

The doctor had her back to us as she administered a yellowish medicine to a waxen-faced youngster. His mother stood guard next to him holding his hand so tight his little fingertips were white.

Without turning Doc Bay said, 'Take a seat, be with you in a while.' She waved a hand at the row of straight-backed chairs on our left. We followed her instructions and waited.

'There, Danny,' she said. 'All done now. The medicine will take a couple of hours to start working but when it does you'll be bright as a new penny.' She ruffled the kid's hair playfully, then turned to his mother. 'Just keep an eye on him over the next day or two, Jenny. I've given you enough medicine to tide you over. If he carries on being sick bring him back and we'll see what we can do for him, OK?'

'Thank you, Doctor. Thank you. How much…?'

She stopped the woman reaching for her

purse. 'You can settle up later. Don't concern yourself now.'

'Oh, thank you.' She took her son by the shoulder and said to him, 'Now, say thank you to the kind doctor, Danny.'

The six year old looked up, eyes big and wide, and was almost on the point of crying but managed to mumble his thanks.

'Just you get better for your ma, you hear?'

Danny bobbed his head up and down. Then Doc Bay turned around and I got my first look at her. I was surprised that she wore spectacles but they suited her. The round glasses seemed to dominate her face but didn't hide the brightness of her blue eyes.

Her honey-blonde hair was tied back into a single pony-tail with a red ribbon. Her face was homely but gave off an air of assurance and she was no taller than five-and-a-half feet but graceful with it.

Pushing the glasses further on her nose she looked at me and smiled. 'Fall off your horse?'

47

'Nope.'

'Stomped on by a mule?'

'Nope.'

'All right – bar fight?'

'Reckon so.'

She shook her head. 'John, why is it that you always bring me the losers?'

Evans laughed. 'Hell, Maureen, he ain't the loser. Cal's the winner.'

She cocked her head to one side and gave me a gleaming smile.

'Sure wouldn't like to be the loser of that one. S'pose I'll be getting him in through the door next.'

'I doubt it, Maureen,' Evans said, obviously enjoying himself. 'Raley'll go back to his ranch and lick his own wounds.'

'Raley, eh?' She seemed impressed, then hooked a finger at me to come over to her desk. I got up a little gingerly because my ribs were really hurting me but I tried to keep the pain from my face. It was no use though; she knew I was hurting.

She said, 'Can you get your shirt off?'

I was a bit offended and replied sharply, 'Sure.'

She folded her arms and watched me struggle out of my vest, then finally out of my shirt. Without a further word she guided me over to the lantern and began her examination. 'Does that hurt? There? There? That's good.' It took a few minutes of gentle poking around before she said that no ribs were broken but that wasn't to say one or two might be cracked, and the bruising was going to be heavy. She then proceeded to rub in some evil-smelling ointment and strapped on a bandage good and tight.

Just her massaging my ribs made me feel good and whenever she bent near me, I could smell wild plums in her hair. The combination of the two made me feel so good I would have fought Raley all over again. But her doctoring wasn't over yet.

'That was the easy part, mister...?'

'Call me Cal, ma'am.'

'OK, Cal. You've got a gash across your cheekbone that'll need some stitches.'

I shook my head. 'No need, ma'am.'

'You're not scared of needles, are you?'

Too damned right I was but I wasn't admitting it so I just shook my head again.

'Don't worry, I won't spoil your good looks if that's what you're worried about.'

John just sat there with a silly grin on his face and I knew that I was beat. I looked into Maureen's face and saw her steely resolve. Shrugging, I gave into her knowing that any further resistance was useless. I was sewn up in a half-hour and I was putting the fee into her hand when she said, 'Come back at the end of the week and I'll remove those stitches.'

Before I knew what I was saying the words were already out of my mouth. 'I got to wait that long to see you?' I could've kicked myself for saying that.

She stood there with a crooked smile on those ripe lips, then said, 'Not unless you need looking after...'

Standing in the doorway of the surgery I felt awkward and tongue-tied. I wanted to say something more but for the life of me couldn't think what. Then it came to me and I said, 'Soapberry.'

Doc Bay was puzzled. 'I'm sorry?'

'You use soapberry.'

'To wash my towels and bandages, yes.'

'Yeah, I reckoned so.'

I guess I surprised her with that little bit of knowledge. She smiled and said, 'See you soon, Cal.'

Her words froze my throat and I could only manage to nod a couple of times. Out on the street Evans dug me in the arm.

'What was all that about, Cal?'

I knew what he was talking about but played dumb. 'What?'

'All that talk about soapberries an' all?'

I tried to dismiss it with a casual wave of my hand but John saw through that. He gave me one of his sly grins and walked on in front mimicking Maureen's voice: 'See you soon, Cal.' And let out a hearty belly laugh.

Billy Joe Brecker was waiting for me outside Dyer's store. He was uneasy and fidgeted in the saddle as we began to ride out of town, heading along the darkening trail back to the ranch.

'Heard about the fight, Will,' he finally said, when we had cleared the town's outskirts. 'Kinda makes me look small, doesn't it?'

'What are you talking about?' I demanded, putting an edge to my voice. 'That was between Raley and me.'

'No it wasn't. Hear tell you took on six of 'em, and beat the hell outta 'em,' Brecker said bitterly. 'I backed down after one hit from Raley alone! Seems to me you just couldn't wait to prove you're a much better man than me. Better with a gun, better with your fists, probably better with women as well.'

Right then I couldn't believe I was hearing a grown man talking like that. I half-hipped in the saddle because I wanted to see Brecker's face, but it was turned away from me.

'Forget that kind of thinking, Billy Joe,' I said in a fatherly sort of way. 'I got busted up a mite in the ruckus. Listen, all men are different. Sometimes it takes six men to break another down, sometimes only one. Doesn't mean a thing. The man it takes six for might faint clean away at the sight of blood. The other *hombre* might be able to walk ten miles after a bronc has stoved in a couple o' ribs. Every man has guts enough for something. Sometimes they're just not always the same thing.'

Brecker was silent a long time and then, as we lifted up on the trail out of the basin said, 'Christine figures me for a coward. A couple of my neighbours, as well. There's Mike Watts of the Box W and Pete Alderson of the Circle A; they won't have anything to do with me, Will. I tried to talk to them back in town, but they ignored me.'

'Forget them,' I advised. 'They'd have been behind you if you'd managed to pull it off and get your cattle back. They left it all to you with nary a one giving you any backing. You lost out and folks never back a loser.'

'No, they're right, Will. I can't cut this life as a rancher. I just don't belong. I haven't got the stomach for it. I'm not only letting myself down, but those at the Leaning B Ranch and Christine.'

'Hell, kid, shake out of it. You'll feel differently about this in the fresh light of morning,' I promised. 'A good night's sleep and a new day'll help. Take my word for it.'

There was no answer from Brecker as he stared ahead.

We didn't speak again until we got to the ranch. I took both horses, stripped off the saddle and gear, wiped them down and gave them a feed of grain and a good drink. I walked into Brecker's ranch house, took the plate of meat and beans Coosie had left out for us and began to eat. As usual the coffee was good, strong and fresh.

I always took my meals in the big house; not that I was being pretentious but it gave the hands a bit of privacy so they could grumble about their boss without having me around. Brecker declined any food but drank a couple of cups of coffee still brooding about the beating he had received from Raley. Nothing I could say would bring him out of his testiness, and when he finished his coffee he fetched out a bottle of Scottish malt whisky and poured himself a healthy slug. I helped him out but drank mine more slowly, appreciating it.

It must have been around midnight when I left the house and joined the others in the bunkhouse. They were all awake and waiting to hear what had happened in town. When I had finished telling them they were downhearted about the outcome. No doubt a couple of them went to sleep with the thought that this was the beginning of the end. The effects of the alcohol, and the punches I had taken soon cocooned me into sleep.

The sun was already up when I awoke, and I cussed. The others were already out on the range, even before the sun had graced the skies, and going about their work. I'm the first to admit that I'm not a cowhand but when I work for someone I like to try and fit into the pattern of my surroundings, sort of blend in with things, but I had overslept and that made me feel bad. After splashing my face with cold water, I dressed and made my way over to the big house.

I went in by the kitchen door and helped myself to a cup of fresh coffee. I nodded a hello to Coosie. He gave me a gap-toothed grin and said that he hadn't seen the boss that morning and would I go fetch him out for breakfast. I carried my cup through to the parlour to seek out Brecker but he wasn't there. The empty whisky bottle lay on its side and I guessed that he must have carried on drinking after I left him.

I moved over to the bedroom door and hammered on it. When there was no reply I turned the handle. The door swung open quietly and I stepped inside. The curtains were closed but enough sunlight filtered into the sparsely furnished room to see. Brecker was still fully dressed sprawled out on the bed.

'C'mon, Billy Joe, rise and shine,' I sang out breezily.

Brecker didn't stir, and there was a smell that was both familiar and disturbing. I moved over to the bed and shook him by the shoulder. There was no movement and fearing the worst I turned him face-up. Blood had dried to a crusty brown around the entry hole in his temple. Where he had used the pillow to muffle the gunshot you could make out the powder burns on it. There was a Colt revolver gripped in his left hand.

I grew cold in the presence of death. My only feeling was to get out of the room. Turning to go I saw his note addressed to me on top of the chest of drawers. I hesitated for a moment before reaching for it, then unfolding it read the neat script.

May 5 1885

This is the last will and testament of William

Joseph Brecker. Being both sound in mind and body I hereby bequeath the Leaning B and all it contains to be shared jointly by my sweetheart, Christine Dyer and the only human being who had faith in me, Will Calhoun.

I blame no individual for what I am about to do, I have surpassed my limitations and cannot go on any further. May God have mercy on my soul and may He bless those whom I leave behind in a country hard on the body and spirit.

William J. Brecker

THREE

I don't think it was the shock of Billy Joe Brecker's death that made me begin to shake – more likely the news on that scrap of paper I was holding in my shaking hands. My mind was blank as to why he should leave any part of the ranch to me. Surely there was someone else more worthy of it? Why didn't he give the whole parcel over to Christine and leave me out of it? It seemed odd to me why he should do that at all.

When I stumbled into the kitchen Coosie took one look at me and knew something was wrong. He set me down at the table, placed a hot mug of Arbuckle's in front of me and left the room. I wrapped both hands around the mug, not bothered about the heat, and looked out of the window but not really looking at anything. I was sitting the same way when Coosie came back in and sat down heavily opposite me. He reached over and took the sheet of paper from my hand, uncrumpled it and read it through.

For a moment his eyes misted up and I thought he was going to shed a tear or two but he didn't; just pulled his shoulders back, swallowed hard and looked at me.

'Jake needs to know about this,' was all he said and left the room.

There were voices out in the yard, then the sound of a horse galloping off. I figured that Coosie had sent a rider to the canyon where Latchford and a few of the hands were branding new calves. The cook came back in, went over to a shelf, and brought down a bottle of whiskey. Without asking he poured out a good measure and handed it me with a command to drink it down. The coffee was lukewarm by now but the whiskey made up for it, and I tossed it down in one go.

There was a moment of silence before I said that someone ought to go and fetch the doctor and Johnny Evans. He agreed and went out again. The initial shock was beginning to wear off now and I knew that I had to get myself together; not for myself but for the men when they returned. Standing in the open doorway and drinking unlaced coffee I watched another rider being dispatched, his horse kicking up clods of earth in its wake as it moved gracefully into a gallop.

I handed Coosie a fresh brew when he came back into the kitchen and said, 'I don't mind admitting that this is one hell of state of affairs.'

'Yeh, jest when the kid was getting himself straight.'

I nodded. 'I really didn't know him. Tell me, was he apt to look on the dark side of things?'

'Suicidal? Nah. Most of the time he kept hisself to hisself but that's nothing new, his uncle was the same.'

'I thought that after he put this DR thing behind him everything would turn out fine. I told him to sleep on it and the next day'd be better.'

'Well, Will, that boy won't see no more mornin's an', let's face facts here, there's still a ranch to be run. An' accordin' to this here will, you're the man in charge now so you got to make up your mind what you're goin' to do.'

'Listen, Coosie, I'm no rancher, I'm a drifter, you know that. 'Sides, half the ranch belongs to Christine Dyer, so she'll have a say in how this place'll be run. I might even give her my half.'

'Over my dead body, sonny!'

I don't know why the idea upset Coosie but the very thought of Christine Dyer taking over the Leaning B got him angry. He banged his cup down on the table and leaned over to me and said, 'Don't sell out to that hell cat! If you do the Leaning B will go belly-up inside o' six months. I'd rather you sell out to Raley or Jonas Ware over Cabin Creek. Leastways there'd still be a job for the crew here.'

I'd never heard Coosie say so much at any one time and what he said gave me food for thought. It seemed that he held a passion about this place and I reckon that one or two others might feel the same way too. But if what he said was true, then I couldn't sell out to Christine but by the same token I didn't want to be tied down to any one place. For the most of my life I'd been around men, horses, towns and women – cows were completely different.

So I said, 'I ain't making any promises but I'll talk to Johnny Evans about the legality of Billy Joe's will first. Then I'll see Christine Dyer to see what she has to say. After that...' I gave a shrug and went out into the fresh air.

It was a little past noon when I spotted the buggy and two riders coming down the ranch road. I tapped out my pipe on the upright and stepped off the porch to greet Doc Bay and Town Marshal Evans. I helped the lady down from the buggy and carried her big valise. I know it sounds silly but I was a little nervous with her – especially after what I had said yesterday. But she was businesslike, wanting to know where Brecker was so I took her through to the bedroom with Evans tagging along.

The Doc went about her examination of the body whilst I explained to Evans all that had happened that morning. He listened but was watching the doc poke, prod and lift Brecker's earthly remains. The whole examination took no more than ten minutes. Then I answered all of his questions leading up to my retiring to bed.

When we stood in the parlour drinking coffee Doc Bay said, 'I'm going to sign the certificate as death by his own hand, Cal. Suicide.'

That sent a little shiver down my spine, her calling me Cal like that. I nodded. She went on. 'If you need a full report, John, I'll write one up and bring it over to your office later.'

'No rush, Maureen,' Evans said softly. 'As far as I know there weren't any kin left, he was the last of the Breckers.'

Maureen nodded, then went out of the

room to wash up and I took the chance to find out about the will and asked Evans about it. He took the note from his pocket, there hadn't been much time to examine it earlier when I handed it to him, and he read it slowly. He sighed and scratched his chin.

'Well, what the law says is,' he said tapping the paper, 'that this will nullifies any other he may have written. It's legal, so I guess that makes you and Christine Dyer partners.'

I had figured that much out for myself but it was better to have it confirmed. Maureen came back into the room and shot me a puzzled look. I didn't know how much she had overheard but more than likely enough. But then all my frustration rose to the surface and I raised my voice.

'I don't want a ranch, John! You know me, I'm a drifter, I've been that way all my life. I don't like things to tie me down.'

John Evans shrugged, waving Brecker's will in the air. 'Half the Brecker spread is yours, Will, says so right here. Maybe Christine'll buy you out.'

'Hell, John! You know I wouldn't want to make any money from Brecker's death! 'Sides, I've already spoken to some of the men and they'd sooner have a greenhorn in charge than a female – don't take offence, ma'am.'

'None taken; then you'll be staying on, Cal?' Maureen asked and I snapped my head up. My turn for being puzzled.

I sighed heavily. I'd backed myself against a wall and had to come to a decision. I tapped the points off on the fingers of my left hand. 'Brecker's given me a half-stake in his ranch, Raley's told me to go, the crew want me to stay and I can't rightly make up my mind. I reckon it all depends on what Christine Dyer has to say.' I threw up my hands in despair.

'I understand, Cal,' she agreed, non-committally.

'Chris might agree to him stayin' on as a working partner,' the town marshal suggested. 'In any case, she's got to be told about Brecker. I'd best get to it. Say, maybe you might want to tag along, Cal, and straighten things out about the ranch and the will.'

I figured that this was as good a time as any to get it out of the way so I agreed. Deep down I was unhappy about the way the whole situation was changing, but what else could I do? I just couldn't ride off and leave everyone up in the air. There were more than twenty men depending on this ranch for their livelihood, and I reckon I had my reputation at stake. Who would hire me after word had gotten out that I had left a whole cow outfit in the lurch? As it happens one of the good things that came out of it was that I was getting the chance to ride alongside Maureen.

Coosie had busied himself in his kitchen knowing that the crews were coming back early and were going to be hungry. He did them, and us, justice with veal pie, potatoes and gravy followed by an upsidedown pie washed down with more coffee. When everyone had gathered, the news broken and the options voiced, all the men agreed to stay on. It had been decided by Jake Latchford, Coosie and a young Texan named Hardtack Watson to bury Brecker alongside his uncle the following day.

It goes without saying that the crew were downcast, most of them hoping that they were going to hang on to their jobs at least until winter when by tradition a few of the hands drifted off. There was some talk of getting back at Raley and his outfit but between Evans and myself we managed to persuade them not to linger on those thoughts.

When we finally finished with Brecker's funeral arrangements it was pushing late afternoon and to get back into town before dark meant we'd have to move ourselves. A Carter buggy's not the fastest thing in the world but Maureen handled it expertly. John Evans and myself rode alongside keeping the pace going at a fair lick.

The shadows were long and dark when we hit Huntings' Main Street. The doctor excused herself and left us to see Christine alone. We found her out back of her store, checking through an inventory of incoming goods, but she stopped when we entered the room. Her gaze swept across me, cold and indifferent, then settled on John Evans a mite warmer.

'John, a pleasant surprise,' she said, ignoring me on purpose. 'What can I do for you?'

Evans looked at one of her assistants and said, 'Is there somewhere more private, Chrissie?'

She frowned at the starpacker's sober tones and the set of his face. She glanced briefly at me but I remained nonchalant. She nodded and led us out of the storeroom and into her own parlour.

She sat in a chair by the fire, John Evans took the only other chair in the room; that left me standing. Evans removed his hat but out of spite I left mine on.

In a way I was glad that the woman was keeping up her hostility towards me, it might help me when I had to make my decisions on Brecker's spread. I don't know why she disliked me so much, I hadn't bad-mouthed her or done anything else of the kind to upset her. But she had acted coldly towards me ever since the day I signed on with the Leaning B. Maybe she resented my intrusion into hers and Billy Joe's life. I don't rightly know, and if the truth be told, I didn't really care.

She said to Evans, 'Tell me what's so mysterious that we have to speak in my parlour, and with *him* here as well?'

I stood there, playing with my belt buckle, happy enough to let the lawman do the talking. As John broke the news of Brecker's suicide I watched the lady for her reaction. For someone receiving bad news about a loved one's death there wasn't a flicker of emotion. Her hands were clasped gently in her lap and there were no tears brimming in her eyes. And she was without a vestige of remorse on her thin face whatsoever. The town marshal could just have well been telling her about the death of some neighbour's dog, she was that dispassionate.

70

Then came the will. And for the first time she showed some emotion.

'You're telling me that this ... this saddle-tramp is getting half of the Leaning B?'

'Cal's no saddle-tramp, Chrissie,' Evans said.

'Like hell!'

I couldn't hold out any longer. 'I don't know what your problem is, lady. I didn't ask for anything from Billy Joe, he just...'

'You took his money sure enough.'

'Of course, he was paying me to protect him.'

'And a fine job you did of that! He's dead, and no thanks to you.'

'For Christ's sake! I was protecting him against Raley and the like, not ... not sleeping in the same bed so he didn't blow his brains out at the first sign of real trouble!'

Evans jumped up between us and waved for calm. 'OK, OK you two, let's keep this civil, yeh?' He turned to Christine saying, 'Look, Chrissie, all I know is that this will is as legal as any piece of documentation as

I've ever seen. Like it or not, you an' Calhoun are partners in the Leaning B. The way you deal with it is up to you two, understand? But I don't like you accusing Cal of not doing his job. You've only got to take one look at the state of Cal's face to see what the boys of the DR did to him yesterday.'

When she looked at me there was a hardness in her eyes combined with a quick, calculating look I've seen on many a gambler's face. She smiled disarmingly and said lightly, 'Listen, Mr Calhoun, I'm sorry about what I said. It was the heat of the moment thing, you know? Billy Joe's death hasn't sunk in yet, I'm still a bit shocked, you do understand?'

Yeah, I understood all right. But she wasn't finished.

'From what I can gather, perhaps it would be the best thing if we could get this business over and done with for everyone's sake at the Leaning B.' She got up and walked over to a small side cabinet, saying over her shoulder,

'Bourbon, gentlemen?'

Her change was so sudden I believed I might have been talking to a stranger. She handed out the drinks saying, 'I've an idea that should be agreeable to us both Mr Calhoun.'

'OK, I'm listening,' I said cautiously.

She said, as though she had just thought of the idea, 'Say, if you were to stay on at the Leaning B as the head boss, looking after the books and such, then I'd be willing to supply all the goods, feed and wages. Well, that is until the end of summer's round-up. By that time we should see how well you can handle the job and what profit there is to be made at the ranch. By then we'd have to renegotiate our contracts.'

'Contracts?' I echoed.

'Of course, Mr Calhoun. Listen, do I have to call you that? Or is there a name you'd prefer?'

'Will is just fine, ma'am.'

'Chrissie is what most folk call me, Will.'

I nodded. ''Bout these contracts, ma'am

… er … Chrissie?'

'If it's fine with you, I'll have my lawyer draw up contracts that legally bind me and you together as co-owners of the Leaning B.'

The town marshal slapped me hard on the shoulder. 'See, Cal, told you that you two would sort things out easily.'

'You did?'

'Sure, I did.' He looked at me askance.

I had the feeling I was being railroaded into something that went way above my head, but I wasn't going to let on. 'Chrissie, when you see your lawyer I'd like to put a clause into them contracts.'

'Clause? Sure, what sort of clause?' She failed to hide the surprise in her voice.

'Just a little proviso that if either one of us should die; get jailed or give up the ranch in any way, then it automatically goes to the other person – no questions asked.'

You could see that my little bit of legal knowledge threw her slightly. She agreed to it after a few seconds of thought and we raised our glasses in a toast to the memory of Billy Joe Brecker.

Also to the success of the Leaning B under its new ownership.

FOUR

By the end of the first week as the 'boss' of the outfit I had worn out one pencil and got a sore thumb and forefinger on my right hand. It felt like me and Coosie had taken an inventory of anything that didn't have four legs and a tail. I had left that up to Jake Latchford because he was the expert. So I sat in the parlour at Brecker's desk, just staring at the ridges of a far-off range knowing that's where I wanted to be. Out there in the open, getting some clean Big Sky air into my lungs.

I dropped the pencil on to the ledger and scrubbed my face with my hand, then got up from behind the desk. The very thought of how anyone could spend a whole day behind one of them things and enjoy it amazed me. I was halfway across the room when there was a knock at the door. I had no time to answer when it opened and in stepped the young Texan, Hardtack Watson, hat in hand.

'Coosie said for me to get you out of the house, sir,' he announced.

'No, don't call me sir. I'll settle for anything but that, OK? I was fixing to go to yonder peaks.' I indicated them with my thumb. Hardtack nodded, I went on, 'Reckon the company'd be appreciated. I'm going crazy talking to them sheets of paper and lines of figures.'

'Coosie's rustled us up some chuck.'

'Sounds great. All right then, let's saddle up and get out of here.'

'Already done, s–'

'It's Will or Cal, OK?'

'Er, sure.'

After a bone-rattling ride of three hours we dismounted on the crest of Moore's Peak, and removed the muslin-wrapped food parcels from our saddlebags. Hardtack went off to find firewood for a big enough fire to brew up some Arbuckle's whilst I ground-tied Tag and Hardtack's big blue roan letting them graze on spring-green grass.

About thirty feet away a pair of pure white mountain goats stood chewing on the grass, their little beady black eyes on me. All the time working the grass in their mouths, watching. Finally they got tired of me and walked a few yards off and began tugging at more sprouts of grass.

It was my first time in this part of the Powder River ridge. As I eased the pains in the small of my back and ribs I looked out over the folds of canyons spreading away in a panorama that left my soul refreshed. It came to me that Nature has a wicked way with her. One minute you get this vista of vast green mesas as far as the eye can see, dotted with grazing cattle; the next she's whipping up a white storm so sudden that you find yourself trapped under a ten, fifteen foot snowdrift. I reckon it's her way of saying that she's still in charge and you got to re-spect that. That's one fight a man can never win. The high country around here is a tough land for those more used to sunnier climes. Winters come early, sometimes as early as the end of September and once the snows have boxed you in, you can count on being stuck inside for a goodly spell. But in summer the heat of the day sucks out all your water and by night the temperature drops enough to make you shiver in your blankets. I once overheard one of the hands asking Hardtack why a Texan should be up here. He said that he was fed up with the south being so draughty and the high country made a change. That was about as close to a man's history you were going to learn – it don't pay to pry too much into a man's past.

Hardtack came back with an armful of broken twigs and thick timber and got the fire going. As we frog-squatted close to the small fire the Texan pulled out his Bull Durham sack, took a leaf out of his prayer book and rolled a smoke. I declined his offer with a little shake of my head, preferring my corn pipe to a rolled cigarette. We didn't exchange one word until we had drunk down our first mug of coffee and devoured the meat pies.

The young Texan stood up and looked down on the trail that our cows had made. I studied his face; his youthful looks were just being marred by the weather. The wind, rain, and sun had tanned his skin a dusky brown, leaving only a muddy forehead when he removed his hat on occasion to mop his brow. He seemed to have been allocated to me by either Coosie or Jake but it didn't matter none to me.

'The cattle are going to water,' he said. 'Best be going along, too.'

That was it. And I thought I could be tight-mouthed but Hardtack beat me hands down at that. It wasn't that he was being unfriendly at all, it was just a cowboy's nature to be sparing with words in the company of a greenhorn. And around cattle that was what I was. But I had him figured to be one of those fellers I'd told Brecker about; the one who shot the loud-mouth dead without saying a word himself.

But when he did start on about cattle he was knowledgeable of the subject and I learned a fair bit from him. On the way up he pointed out to me that the cattle had their own way of doing things. On the flat land near the river our men put salt blocks out so that the cows could get the mineral after watering, then they made their bed-grounds later in the day. The blocks also attracted deer and they in turn added a variation to the rest of the crew's diet. Coosie was meant to make one hell of a venison stew.

We tightened the cinches of our saddles, mounted up and began searching around the peak just to see if all the cattle that had been grazing there were heading down to the water. We were also on the lookout for a few calves that we were missing. He pointed out two of the 'slick-ears' near their mothers and said he was pleased that the grass looked good and come summer should fill out the cattle ready for market. Looking back up to the ridge the goats had gone.

Jake and a handful of men were in another canyon branding calves. You could hear and smell where they were before you ever got to see them. Bleating-calves, bellowing cows and the acrid aroma of charred hair greeted us as we rode closer to the camp. We came down off the trail pushing a couple of calves in front of us, and as we rounded the bend up ahead of us were three corrals. There was one large one stoutly made of ponderosa pine logs and on either side were smaller but equally strong-looking corrals. Hardtack cut the calves into one of the smaller corrals and waved me over to behind the big one.

We off-saddled and tied our horses along with the others at the rope picket, letting them blow for a while. We headed over to where Jake and a thickset cowboy named Lars Jensen, a Swede by birth but cowboy at heart, were heating up a couple of running irons in a fiercely burning fire. Jake looked up and called me over.

'Ever branded a calf, Will?' he asked.

'Can't say I ever have.'

He wagged his head. 'OK, I'll show you the first 'un an' you can do the next.'

'If you think I'm up to it.'

He shot me a steel-eyed look that said I'd better be. Jake took out a heavy-bladed knife and examined its edge, then, resheathing it said, 'For ear markin'.' He crossed the corral to an upright, took down his rope and shook out a loop. Swinging it expertly above his head a couple of times he threw it at a calf about fifteen feet away, and caught it by both hind legs. The way he did it looked so easy. I just hoped that he didn't expect me to be as good or anywhere as good as him.

Jake threw the calf, bunching its hind legs together and hauled out a length of pigging string from his back pocket. I was leaning up against the snubbing post in the middle of the corral when there was one almighty *thump!* I was almost knocked off my feet by the impact of a half-ton cow charging me.

'Jake! What the hell's going on?'

'Stand still!' he yelled.

I looked over my shoulder and saw the

cow backing off, shaking great globules of saliva as it shook its massive, ugly head. She was snorting loudly and began to paw the ground. I knew she was going to have another try at me. The cow lowered her head, her horns looking long and evil this close and charged again. *Crunch!*

The snubbing post took the full force again and a pair of horns appeared on either side of me.

'Shoot it, Jake!' I yelled.

'Stay where you are, goddammit!' he yelled back.

'For Christ's sake – shoot her!' My voice had risen a couple of octaves by now, and I'm not afraid to admit that I was scared bad now.

Hardtack and Swede suddenly appeared at my side, waving their hats in the air, yipping at the cow, distracting her from charging at me again. I didn't know if the snubbing post would take any more punishment from the cow and it was something I could do without finding out.

Jake quickly finished tying off the bleating calf, who was emulating her mother in giving Jake a hard time, her legs thrashing out wildly. But he had her tied and threw open the gate to the big corral where the placid cattle were. The cow saw her way of escaping from the two wild men yelling at her and made a run for it. Jake helped her along by whipping his rope above her head and hauled the gate to when she was in.

He turned to me and everything on his heavily moustached face suggested that he was going to give me a dressing down but he busted out laughing instead. The others who had witnessed the event joined in. Especially Hardtack and Swede. It wasn't long before I saw the funny side of it and joined in.

After that they didn't give me a moment's rest all afternoon. Everyone took the chance to rib me about what happened in the corral. I was going to be 'posted elsewhere', or 'take the problem by the horns', and even 'shoot anything that had four legs', you know the kind of thing. And the good part about it all was that every word spoken was in good humour, not one voiced with malice.

So I figured that this was the turning point where the crew of the Leaning B came to accept me as their new boss.

It hadn't taken gunplay or an act of heroism to gain their respect. They could see that I was doing my best for all of them, and I reckoned they were more impressed with that than anything else I could have done. Perhaps my fight with Raley *did* have something to do with it but deep down I hoped that wasn't so.

From now on, I told myself, I had to turn my attention on keeping the Leaning B going and the crew employed. I had been watching them and they were hard workers, each and every one of them seasoned cowboys – right down to the teenager, Hardtack Watson. You could see why they held Jake Latchford in high esteem and I hoped that his opinion of me had changed since we first met. In fact, he was the first to start the ribbing, which was a good sign.

Night was crowding in and all but a handful of calves had been branded. The men were working by the light of the fire. Hardtack came over to where I was feeding sticks into the branding fire and suggested that we had best make our way back to the ranch with Coosie. The cook had packed everything but the coffee pot into his chuck wagon.

I felt reluctant to leave what I thought of as a magical canyon. It had been such a long time since I had felt such contentment. I also knew that there should also be some kind of distance between me and the men, so I hesitantly agreed.

'These figures don't tally,' I said to Coosie as we sat in his kitchen drinking coffee and munching on fresh-baked biscuits. The morning sun was already bright and streamed in through the opened doorway. The air buzzed with flies and other winged insects. The ranch was quiet as the crew had already left to finish off the branding back at the canyon, leaving me and Coosie at the ranch.

'Here,' I pushed the paper at him. 'Take a gander at them figures for me will you?'

'Hell, Cal! Book work is like talkin' Chinee to a mule to me but I'll give it my best.' He took the paper and ran a nail-bitten finger across the columns. I drank my belly-wash and looked out across the yard, waiting.

'Hah, hah! There you are.' He stabbed his forefinger at the offending culprit. He twisted the sheet around so I could read it.

The figure read: *$600,00 for three Holstein bulls and six Hereford cows.*

It was the amount missing from Brecker's account, but I couldn't find the bill of sale to reconcile those figures. I thought about it for a moment before asking, 'They wouldn't be the ones in town that Raley had put into quarantine, would they?'

'Could well be, Cal. Though I couldn't rightly say. I don't get involved with any-thing outside of my kitchen on this ranch.'

89

I nodded then said, 'What with all that hullabaloo over Billy Joe's death and the like, them critters went clear out of my mind. It must be them, but where's the bill of sale gone?'

Coosie shrugged. 'You carry on studyin' them figures and you'll finish up chuckleheaded as a prairie dog!'

I had to agree with him on that point. I said, 'I guess the only thing for me to do is ride into town and sort things out with Johnny Evans.' He took one long look at me knowing what was coming next. 'Then I'll pay Mrs Dyer a visit and hand over these papers.'

Coosie switched places from beside the pot-belly stove to the doorway. Standing with his back to me he spat out a stream of cuss words so heated it made him mad enough to make some up that even I've never heard. He must have gone on for minutes before he ever stopped to draw breath and I managed to ask him what was wrong with her.

'She ain't got a good bone in her body. She's a bad 'un, Cal. You take my word for it.' He spoke the words in a voice as frosty as a November night.

'What has she done to make you hate her so much?'

He turned to look at me and his face was blank. He went back to the range and started slapping some flour around. I guessed that was as far as I was going to get with him. It got me to thinking that somewhere along the line she must have hurt him, and hurt him bad. But that was his affair, not mine.

Standing outside I breathed in deep and held it for a while. Brecker's office may have been fine for a city-bred feller but you can't beat a good shot of Big Sky air, and that's a fact. I was dressed only in shirt-sleeves, and there was a bite to the wind as she came off the ridge that made me shiver.

I couldn't believe my ears. Arriving in town I'd ridden straight over to Evans's office to see about reclaiming the Leaning B cattle.

And he was sitting there telling me that they were gone. Sold on.

I was fighting mad and began taking it out on John.

'What in hell's name do you mean, they're sold? Who sold 'em? Who bought 'em? God-dammit, they're *my* cattle! No one's got the right to sell 'em...'

'Whoa up, Will!' Evans held up his hands. 'I only know that they were let out of quarantine sometime at the beginning of the week. I weren't in town at the time...'

'That's convenient.'

Evans's face hardened. 'Meanin'?'

'You turn your back and my cattle take a passeur.'

'You son-of-a-gun, just listen to yourself, will you?'

But the blood was thundering in my ears making me deaf to his words. 'You said yourself that you're not going to be around for too much longer!' I shouted back at him. 'So why bother yourself with a couple of cows being sold off, especially when they don't belong to you?'

Evans jumped up, knocking his chair over. He leant across the table and wagged a finger in my face. His own had turned an angry red. 'If you weren't a friend, Will, I'd knock you down on your ass – don't think twice that I wouldn't! You just shut that leaky mouth awhile and *listen!*'

He moved around the desk and stood in front of me, hands stuffed deep in his pockets. Probably doing that to stop himself from hitting me. 'Them cows have been sold on to someone else, that's true enough. But I don't know who bought 'em or who sold 'em – hand on my heart. A moment ago I thought we were friends.'

'Well, we still are.'

'Are we?' He shook his head slowly and said, 'A friend don't go around accusin' another of betrayin' him.'

'I'm … I'm sorry, John,' I managed to murmur. What else was there to be said? Evans remained quiet, his jaws working hard quelling his anger.

The office grew still, only the sounds of the town outside filtered in. The town marshal stood there with the sun reflecting off the badge pinned to his vest, staring me squarely in the eyes. Waiting to see if something was going to happen.

We must have stood there like that for all of five minutes. Brooding silence and eyes alert. The anger in me began to slowly ebb and the red mist that had clouded my judgement began to disappear. When the rage had finally passed I realised what a fool I had been ever to accuse John of being in cahoots with those who had taken the cattle. I had to say so.

'I reckon on being a fool, John.' I stretched out my hand. 'Shake on it and accept my apologies?'

Evans accepted and grinned. 'No hard feelin's, Will.'

As we shook hands the tension seemed to disappear.

'I need to find out about them critters, John,' I said.

'Sure. I'm with you on that.'

'So, where do we start?'

He scratched at the heavy stubble on his lower face. 'I'll go to the stockyard an' ask around a couple of them cattle detectives. They owe me a favour or two.'

'OK, what about me?'

'You? You go see Christine about the ranch, after all she is your partner.'

'Yeh, don't remind me.'

Evans moved across the room and strapped on his double-rigged outfit and took down a scattergun from the rack. He checked that all the weapons were loaded and ready for use. I raised a quizzical eyebrow.

'To serve and protect, Will,' he said as a way of explanation. 'I'm serving the community and protecting myself.'

We stopped at the door and before going out onto the street John put a restraining hand on my forearm. 'Whatever happens, Will, let me deal with any trouble, yeah?'

'Trouble? What trouble?'

'You usually go off half-cocked. Remember that time in Billings with that gambler feller?'

I recalled that incident very clearly but that's a whole story in itself, and I didn't want John dragging up the past again. I said, 'Sure, John. But that ain't gonna happen … I hope.'

'Too damned right it ain't!' Evans growled. 'This is my town and my people. We do it my way. Be sure you understand that.'

Evans gave me no choice and I nodded.

'Meet me at Joe's Café around one o'clock,' he said, then was out on the street striding away towards the stockyards.

I was early for our meeting and sat in the café eating steak pie with potatoes swimming in a gooey thick gravy. Being so hungry I forgot the taste and wolfed it down. The place was busy with lunchtime trade and I was sharing the table with two others. One was a stockman and the other a visiting sales rep from New York City. When he spoke his harsh nasal accent grated on my ear. It was all I could do to stay sitting at the table with him.

There was a wedge of soggy apple pie and a fresh coffee in front of me when John Evans entered the room. The set of his face told me that he was no bearer of good tidings. The men sharing the table were only halfway through their dessert when Evans arrived.

He stood with his shoulders squared back and lips pressed into a thin line. The men ignored him.

'Excuse me, gents,' he said softly.

But they went right on eating.

He leant across the table and, much to their surprise, picked up their plates and took them over to the serving counter. The New Yorker stood up and demanded, 'What the hell d'you think you're doin'?'

Evans said, 'Finish it off in the kitchen.'

But the New Yorker wasn't having none of that and advanced on Evans. 'You've got no right, mister! Put that food back and I mean right now!' Clearly he was blind to the star on Evans's chest.

The peace officer gave him no chance. He swung the barrel of his scattergun in an arc that ended at the Easterner's temple. He went down like a felled redwood and stayed there. The stockman had recognised John and made no objection. He simply looked down at the unconscious man and said, 'If he wanted to eat sawdust, he should've gone over to Abraham's to eat.' Then stepped over him on the way out.

Evans sat down. 'How'd it go with Christine?'

I shrugged. 'Much as I expected, really. She looked the paperwork over, thought the ranch was doing well and questioned me about the money spent on them cows.'

'She say anything about them?'

'Such as?'

'Well, where they were or the such?'

Again I shrugged then said, 'Can't say she did. You gettin' at something, John? Do you know something?'

He leant back in his chair and tipped his

hat to the back of his head. 'I'll get right down to it. Dave Raley bought them cows on Wednesday last. Paid the vet two hundred dollars and got a bill of sale from him.'

I was poleaxed.

Evans continued. 'I found out that the vet made Brecker sign a release document that gave them over into his care, to see fit to do whatever he felt he had to with them. I read the document, and even though some of the reading is mighty ambiguous, it's legal.'

I had to think about that for a moment then something clicked. 'You mean to say that when I rode into town with Brecker to face Raley, them cattle belonged to a pox-ridden vet who's probably working for Raley?'

'Keep your voice down, Will.'

I was that mad I hadn't realised that I had begun to shout.

Evans said, 'But you are right, Will. Old Doc Weatherly was the true owner from the time Billy Joe put his signature on that piece of paper.'

I banged a fist down on the table. The

noise made a few diners look up; others pointedly looked away or took a keen interest in the contents of their plates.

'I ain't going to let this go,' I seethed.

'You've got no choice.'

'Haven't I? Just you watch me.'

FIVE

There was a strange glow in the room even though my eyes were shut. Sleep hadn't come easily that night and I figure that I must have downed a half-pint of whiskey before climbing gratefully into bed.

But for what seemed like hours I was tossing and turning unable to get to sleep because all I could think about was Dave Raley buying up those cows.

It was warm even though I'd kicked off the blanket, and I put my light-headedness down to the drink. A loud noise from somewhere in the house echoed away into the night followed by a wave of heat sweeping over me but all I wanted to do was lie there and try to sleep.

Someone was calling out my name, and tugging urgently at me, trying to wake me.

The voice sounded far off, like it was coming from one end of a canyon and bouncing off the walls towards me. A picture of the canyon where we had been branding yesterday came to my mind's eye and I was there again. It was the heat from the branding fires that was making me feel warm, and the stench from burning hide made me feel light-headed. I didn't want to leave that place; it was comfortable but the tugging persisted. The sudden shock of water slapping me in the face made me come awake instantly.

I wasn't in the canyon, after all. I was in Billy Joe's bedroom and it was full of smoke. Thick and broiling like thunderheads. I gasped for some air but sucked down a lungful of acrid smoke that made me cough violently. I struck out blindly. My hand connected with a body and I grabbed for it. Coosie shouted in my ear, 'We're on fire! Got to get out, boy!'

Jumping out of bed I began groping around for my boots.

'Ain't got the time to get anythin'!' Coosie

shouted again. 'Everythin's alight back there! Somebody's tryin' to burn us out! Just get your hide outa here! Leave everythin' behind!'

He grabbed me by the arm, and led me out of the room into the parlour. A wall of flame streaked out before us like a Gila monster's tongue and we were forced back into the small bedroom. Coosie managed to slam the door behind us, blocking out the heat. It gave us precious time to think, and to get our breath back. Thick black clouds of smoke swirled all around, and Coosie gave in to a coughing fit that must have hurt his ribs. Inhaling all the dense smoke was making mine ache again.

Knowing time was short I desperately looked around. I pulled the cook around by the arm and pointed to the window. He understood what I meant to do, and between us we lifted an upright chair and threw it at the window. The glass shattered all about, and a welcome blast of fresh air hit us, though it was only going to be a brief lull.

Pushing me forward Coosie yelled, 'You go first, son. I'll be right behind you.'

I shook my head. 'No, you might need a leg up...'

'I ain't a-arguin'. Get out of here – now!'

He pushed me so hard I half fell out of the shattered window frame. I scrabbled to my feet and turned to help the old man climb out. From somewhere at the back of the house there came a very loud *bang!* I looked on in horror as the bedroom door was blown off its hinges, and tossed across the room as easily as a cowboy would throw a rope.

I was gripping Coosie's hands, ready to pull him through to safety when he turned towards the sound. A blown-apart section of the door hurtled across the room towards us. It struck him across the throat. I heard the sickening sound of crunching bones above the crackle and hiss of flames. Coosie's hands were jerked from mine, and his body was tossed backwards, crashing against the window frame. He hung there, unable to fall down because he was pinned up by jagged wooden stakes, like someone had crucified him.

Oblivious to the heat prickling my flesh I was transfixed by the scene. Hands began dragging at me – pulling me away and I was thrown to the ground. I tried to fight them off but I was in no condition to defeat them, I simply gave in.

After I had woken it took a few moments to realise where I was. The room was dark save the glow from an oil lamp set low. I lay there and let my eyes adjust themselves to the dimness of the bunkhouse. The harsh rasping sound of men snoring peppered the otherwise stillness. My first attempt to move brought out an unintentional groan. Pain shot across my ribs, hard and fast. Taking it easier the next time around I managed to push myself upright and looked around.

The lamp was set in the middle of a small table where Hardtack Watson and Jake Latchford sat idly reading through a couple of battered catalogues. A couple of other bunks were empty and I guessed that these men must have pulled night duty. The Texan looked over and seeing I was awake nudged his foreman with a toepoint. They both rose and sauntered over.

Hardtack pulled over a chair and straddled it. 'Want a drink?' he asked.

'Yeh,' I said. My voice sounded like rusty metal.

He drew a cupful of water from a nearby bucket and gave it to me. It tasted the sweetest of drinks after a long drought and I finished it in one go. As I put the cup down I noticed the back of my hand was covered in white, puss-filled blisters. The other was, too.

'How long have I been out?'

Jake answered. 'A couple of nights.'

'Coosie … is he?'

Jake hesitated. 'Dead,' he said softly. 'If the door didn't kill him then the fire would have finished him. We were lucky to be round that side of the house where you and Coosie were escaping. You were out but the flames beat us back from rescuing Coosie. We just couldn't get to him...'

'Them flames sure travelled quick-like through the whole place,' Hardtack said.

Jake nodded and began to roll a smoke. When he had lit up he said, 'Someone poured oil all around the place. Reckoned that he wanted to make a good job of it. To tell you the truth, I think it was you he was after, Cal. He didn't allow for Coosie being up and working in his kitchen.'

The idea of someone trying to kill me in cold-blood sent a small shiver of fear down my spine. I looked up and said, 'Did you manage to find any tracks?'

Hardtack nodded. 'Yeah, but they petered out when we hit O'Fallon Creek.'

'That ain't far from DR land, is it?' I asked.

'Sure ain't.'

There was a brief minute's silence as I examined my burns. 'All right,' I said. 'At first light we'll saddle up and pay Mister Raley a visit. The man's got a whole passel of questions that need answering.'

Jake paced up and down, drawing deep on the quirly. Finally he stopped, turned and looked me in the eye and said, 'Me and the men are behind you on this one, Cal. We may not look much but there ain't a man here who won't fight alongside you.'

His words were as good as any medicine and that sparked a well of good feeling inside of me. Jake Latchford was twenty-nine, of small build with dark broody eyes but at that moment he had pulled himself upright and stood ten feet tall. I caught the light in his eyes and knew that here was a man who I could really trust; or to coin the Southern phrase, to ride the river with. A man born in the saddle whose word wasn't given lightly or that often, but once given would be seen out to the death. He gave a curt nod then went back to the small table and the wish-book.

Dawn couldn't come quickly enough for me. I had spent the awakening hours stripping down and oiling my gun, made awkward by the burns but something I suffered. As I carried out this essential chore I let my mind wander. I got around to thinking about how things around me had changed ever since I took on the Leaning B. I also knew that I was changing along with it. I was now running, or co-running, a small outfit with men dependent on my judgement. Add to this the troubles with our neighbouring rancher Dave Raley, plus the murder (yes, I did say murder) of our cook and I reckon that was enough obligation for anyone.

I made a vow to myself that I would see this situation right through to the end – whatever the outcome. There was too much at stake and I wasn't prepared to be railroaded by anyone. As I said to Jake, Raley had a lot to answer for. He seemed to be behind everything that had happened to the Leaning B of late. But to be fair to the man, I couldn't blame the fire and Coosie's death on him. Well, not yet anyhow. Not without evidence. I'd have to wait and see what daylight would bring.

The early morning mist hung over O'Fallon Creek, moving spectrally with the motion of the water. Twenty-eight mounted, and well-armed riders brought their cow ponies to a halt at the water's edge. The riders let the ponies dip their muzzles into the cold water whilst they remained silent in their saddles. They used the halt to relax and roll themselves smokes – either out of sheer habit or anxiousness. There were those who looked capable of handling a side arm or rifle but there were others whose only use for a handgun was for knocking in nails.

The DR ranch began on the opposite side of the creek and stretched down to Cottonwood Creek. It was almost three times the size of the Leaning B that spread from this side of the creek, back to the Powder River and over to the ridge. Jake and Hardtack had already been on DR land looking for the murderers' tracks. Seeing as they knew where we were heading it saved us a lot of time. But knowing that once we forded the creek and were on DR land progress would be slower.

I puffed on an old corn pipe I borrowed from Swede as I looked at the golden trees on the opposite bank swaying in the wind. In fact, nearly everything I was wearing belonged to Swede. He was about the same height and build as me and let me borrow some gear. The gun and holster was a spare belonging to Johnny Lowman, a small bearded man good around cows.

Still no one had uttered a word. Even the ponies were well behaved. I guess that there just wasn't much to be said. The men knew what we had planned and each knew what was expected of them.

Jake had already explained that if they came across any of the cattle Brecker had quarantined they were to be brought home. If they came across any other cattle, branded or not, they were to be left alone. He assigned Swede, Dick Hassell and his son to cut out our cattle. The rest of us were to ride on to Raley's house and settle things with him.

Jake looked fine in his get-up, a Montanan cowboy right down to the woolly chaps and large rowelled spurs. On his right hip he carried a Remington that seemed well cared for, and a Winchester carbine in the saddle boot. He stood up in the stirrups and waved his arm forward. His cow pony led off at a walk and the others fell in line behind him.

Once in the creek the water splashed over our boots – cold but welcoming. We had disturbed a school of paddlefish and they darted crazily out of our path. Some of the men seemed fascinated by the sight but I was more engrossed in watching the trees ahead of us.

They grew close enough to hide a small band of men intent on ambushing us if they wanted.

I gathered up the reins in my left hand, flicked off the restraining hammer thong to my holster and eased the pistol in its leather. It was easy enough to be lulled into a feeling of well-being but I remained alert for any danger. We were making a lot of noise as we crossed the creek but it was unavoidable, and hoped that it wasn't being carried too far. Jake climbed the bank first and pulled over to the right.

Soon all the riders were back on firm land and gathered around their foreman. He leant on the saddlehorn and said, 'I reckon you want to listen from Cal from hereon. I got you this far but I'm no leader when it comes to this kind of thing. Cal will take the front and you'll take your orders from him. That clear?'

I thanked Jake and told the men to be careful and not to do anything stupid. 'All we're here for is to get back what rightly belongs to Leaning B and when that's done I'll sort out Raley.'

'Sort him out good an' proper,' Dick Hassell called out.

'If there's any gunplay, Dick, make sure you shoot the other man and not one of your own, OK?' Jake said jokingly.

'No need to tell me that,' he mumbled, upset by the jibe. That got me wondering as to how many Hassell may have mistakenly shot in the past.

'That goes for any of you,' I pointed out. 'I'd like to see no guns used at all but that might be impossible. But, like I say, if there is, make your shots count, understand?' There was a chorus of agreement and we were heading off north-east again. Riding up front I soon had Hardtack alongside me for company. The Texan was sign reading like an Indian and curiosity got the better of me.

'Who taught you to read sign?'

He gave a little shrug of his massive shoulders and said, 'Back home there was a guy called Jesus. He was half Comanche, half Mexican an' he used to work for my pa sometimes. When I was a kid he used to take me ridin' up around Eagle Pass. That was some country to a yonker – wild and dangerous. He showed me how to track down game for our supper and never failed the oncet. I soon got the hang of it.'

I knew that country well and nodded. It was a notorious haven for badmen where violence was an everyday happening. 'Is tracking men any different?' I asked.

He thought about it for a moment, then said, 'They think they're different – men. They reckon to being more devious than a cougar but they ain't. Man's nothing but an animal hisself and there weren't no one who could escape from Jesus.'

'What d'you mean?'

Hardtack was silent for a minute, and in the background the sound of the creek could still be heard above the soft cropping of horses.

'The US Army hired him to recapture deserters from time to time. Even made him cross over into Mexico to get them back. He didn't like it but they had something over him and he did whatever they wanted.'

The bitterness crept into the Texan's voice mixing with the adoration that Hardtack had for the half-breed. For a Texan to be friends with a man of such mixed blood was a rare thing and coming from such a young man it was rarer still.

'You ever hear from him?' I asked.

'He died in Mexico a few years back. Word was that he was killed going after some Mexican banditos running cattle over the Rio Grande. That's a crock of shit! There ain't no man alive who could've crept up on old Jesus without him knowin' it!'

It began to rain as we rode deeper on to DR land. Fine at first but it quickly turned into a downpour as black thunderheads churned up the sky overhead. The cow ponies were well trained and obeyed the riders' commands. Unfortunately my horse Tag wasn't, and I had a devil's own time in controlling him. At the first crash of thunder he was off and I had to hold on for all I was worth. It was almost as black as night and we were galloping across unfamiliar ground. The fear of being pitched or losing Tag was gut-wrenching. A bolt of lightning lit up the land and suddenly there was a giant tree only yards in front of me, and Tag was heading straight for it.

I sang out a string of curses as I fought to

steer my horse from colliding with the tree. It was only at the last moment that he swerved and we went over, slipping on the wet ground. Arms and legs, hooves and saddle gear went end over end as we pitched across the land.

I could feel the pain return to my damaged ribs as I came to a skidding halt against the bole of a tree. For a moment I was seeing double of everything and I shook my head to clear it.

'You should get yourself a proper horse, Cal,' Jake Latchford said easily.

I looked up at the ramrod and nodded. I couldn't manage anything else right at that time. Jake reached down and hauled me to my feet. Someone had gotten hold of Tag and brought him over to me. I quickly examined him and was surprised that he hadn't been injured at all. I checked that I still had my pistol, thankful that it was there. Breathing a sigh of relief I remounted, biting back the pain from my ribs.

The rain continued to lash down and soak

everything in sight. I leaned over to Latchford and said, 'This weather's not going to
help us.'

'Not one bit,' he replied.

'Any chance of shelter?'

'Nope.'

'Damn it! I ain't turning back now.'

'Listen, this could work for us,' Jake said
raising his voice against the noise of the
wind. 'It'll cover us as we get further on to
DR land without any of them rannies spot-
ting us. I reckon the men'll take cover in a
line shack or under some makeshift tent.
They ain't ones to be riding the range in this
weather.'

'I hope to God you're right about that.
The last thing we need is to ride up on top
of some jumpy rannies who'll start a shooting match.'

As Jake shook his head water ran off his
hat in big globules. 'We didn't come out
here for a picnic.'

'I know,' I interrupted. 'The less gunplay,
the better for everyone, though.'

Jake grunted in agreement.

'OK, then. Let's be on our way.'

The order went out to move on and hooves splashed through the mud. No one had voiced any complaints and we moved off without a further word.

We spent the next hour riding through the downpour heading further on to DR land without coming across man or beast. The men searched the area for any cattle or rannies but nothing could be found. Rain hammered down on my hat beating an incessant tattoo. I was soaked through to the bone and no doubt every other man was too.

Then there was a break in the clouds as the wind picked up and after a very violent downpour the rain began to ease up. The sun broke out from behind the clouds and before long we were being dried off under a much welcome heat.

The only trouble is when that kind of heat hits, it makes you tired. And everyone was drowsy. Sluggish enough to almost miss a small herd of cattle moving slowly near a stand of trees. Swede spotted them first and called everyone's attention to them. The men became alive and automatically began to do what they did best – cowboying.

I reined in and watched them go about their business with a slight twinge of jealousy that I wasn't going to admit to. Their mounts kicked up great clods of earth that matted their woollen chaps, changing their colour to a dark and dirty brown. It didn't take them long to cut out those cows that had once been bought by Brecker.

As agreed, Dick Hassell and Swede with four others were to drive the cattle back to our land whilst the rest of us rode to Dave Raley's ranch house to sort out our problems. We sat and watched them ride off with two of the Herefords and three Holsteins. There wasn't much daylight left to go looking for more – we had to come back another time.

I was beginning to hurt as my ribs protested against the punishment they were getting. Johnny Lowman saw this and told me to dismount. He dug around in his saddlebags and came out with a roll of bandage.

'Lift up your shirt,' he ordered.

I did as I was told. He quickly wound the wide bandage around my body and gave a good tug for extra measure, then tied it off.

'That should see you through,' he said and remounted.

I nodded my thanks and kicked my horse forward. Lowman had made a good job of it and although it was tight, the bandage helped me somewhat. My time with the hands of the Leaning B had given me a quick education in the prowess of cattlemen. I knew that they knew their way around cows, but now I knew that they had to be almost self-sufficient. A town could be more than a day's ride away; a neighbour no closer than a hundred miles, so he couldn't rely on anyone else but himself. He was his own man. That is why townsfolk, myself included at one time, always thought of them as a surly bunch of critters.

We heard the report of the gunshot ahead of us before the sound of fast approaching horsemen. We were in a shallow dip so that gave the gunmen the advantage of higher ground. I saw the flash of another weapon, high and to my right. The slug fell well short of its target. I hauled out my own Winchester carbine and worked the lever. Without really aiming I sent a returning shot.

The attacker had anticipated that and had moved position. He fired again and this time it was closer. Amongst the Leaning B men most of them had their weapons out, scanning the upper slope for other riders.

A horse and rider came into view a way to the left and two of our men fired simultaneously. They missed but it made the gunman swerve and change direction. Johnny Lowman turned his horse around and pulled the carbine out of the scabbard. Quickly and expertly, he fired off three rapid shots. The fleeing gunman's horse shuddered with the impact as the bullets found their mark and passed through its flanks. The mount faltered in its stride but carried on for a couple of yards before its hind legs gave way and then collapsed to the ground. The rider was thrown off landing heavily on his backside.

'That man sure can fly!' Lowman yelled. His attention was concerned with more on-coming fire, but he sat out in the open calmly pushing more shells into the Winchester's magazine. One or two of the hands watched him and shook their heads in silent appraisal.

Jake Latchford, working hard the lever of his own Winchester shouted, 'I think we got a welcoming committee, Cal!'

Looking at him, I said, 'You don't say?'

More shots were aimed at us and since we were in a dip we were easy targets. 'We got to get out of here!' I shouted.

'Got to agree with you there, Cal,' Hardtack said. 'We better make a run for the river.'

'You figure our horses to make it?' asked Jed Briggs, our wrangler.

'You'll soon find out if that little filly of

yourn has got the bottom or not,' Hardtack replied.

A volley of fire sent gouts of mud showering our horses' hooves. It was time for the talking to stop and I slapped Tag across the rump with my carbine. The others were quick to follow my lead.

Gunshots boomed in our wake, cutting through the empty air.

We put spurs to horseflesh and demanded more from our horses than we had the right to. But they seemed to sense the danger and gave us what majestic strength they had to give.

We rode hard for two or more miles before finally catching up with our party. I quickly blurted out what was happening and told them to ride on. I pointed to Hardtack and told him to stay with me before ordering the others to ride on ahead.

'Me and Hardtack'll buy some time,' I explained. 'We'll delay 'em long enough for you to get to O'Fallon Creek. I don't think they want a stand up fight – I hope.'

'Then I'll stay with you,' Jake ventured.

'No, you won't. If anything happens to me, you're in charge, yeh?'

Jake didn't like it much being told to walk away from a fight but he had the sense enough not to argue at a time like this. We heard hoofbeats in the distance, followed by the occasional gunshot. Finally the ramrod got mounted and led the rest of the crew away. Hardtack and I stood in the open like targets in a shooting gallery.

'Well, Hardtack,' I said. 'It's ye an' me.'

'Sure looks like that way.'

'I figure on leading them away from Jake and the boys, say over to that stand of timber, yonder.'

Hardtack nodded.

'That way we can have us some cover and stand 'em off a little easier.'

He nodded again. 'Sure, you're callin' the shots.'

We pushed our mounts into a canter, to make sure the oncoming rannies knew exactly where we were. Once they had spotted us they changed direction and rode hell for leather towards us. I looked back and saw the leading riders and recognised Dave Percy and Brian Gillman amongst them. They must have seen me as they turned their heads towards each other and waved their men on.

Once inside the timberline we jumped off our horses and hobbled them. Hardtack pulled out a box of cartridges and dropped them on the floor between us. We took cover behind a large deadfall and poked the carbine barrels over the top. The Texan's weapon boomed. A horse reared up, screeching in a high-pitched whinny. He fired again. The horse went down in a heap of dead equine flesh.

The rider had managed to jump clear of the stirrups and run away.

But the others came on.

The air was soon filled with the report of heavy-calibre rifle fire and the lighter crack of handguns. Gunsmoke lay thick and almost tangible in the still air as we both laid down volley after volley of hot lead. Wood splinters peppered the air and I ducked down behind the log to reload and catch my breath. When I reloaded, Hardtack followed my example and I held the DR rannies off. A minute or so later the returning fire became wide spaced, then there wasn't a sound to be heard.

Taking a chance, I raised my head above the deadfall and looked out. Apart from the horse Hardtack had shot in the opening seconds there was nothing else to be seen. Me and Hardtack exchanged puzzled looks and fully reloaded our weapons. The silence was deafening to the ears. We waited for a full five minutes, my nerves were stretched to the limit. Just waiting for a surprise attack but it never came.

'You reckon they've gone?' Hardtack whispered.

A shrug of my shoulders was all he got for a reply.

'Want to take a look-see?'

'Be my guest.'

Hardtack cautiously got to his feet, the carbine extending out in front of him, and walked around the deadfall. He dodged nimbly behind a tree. There was no gunfire. He worked his way to a clearing and stood there listening. Finally he turned and said, 'It's all clear, Cal. They must've high-tailed it.'

I got up from our hiding place, still watchful for any enemy and headed over to where the Texan stood. It was true, there was no sign of any of the DR rannies to be seen. I leant against the tree and used my shirt sleeve to wipe the sticky sweat from my forehead.

'We best get back after the boys,' I said.

SIX

The town marshal was the last person I expected to see when we arrived back at the ranch. But he was there and so was Doc Bay. I hadn't really thought about her over the last day or so but seeing her again made something bunch up tight in the pit of my stomach, and hold it there for a minute. John Evans was leaning against a corral post, smoking a cigar and studying the burnt-out remains of the big house. I handed my set of reins to Hardtack and sauntered over to the lawman.

'Hiddy, John.'

'Cal.'

He waved a hand at the house. 'Care to tell me what happened?'

I took off my hat and ran a hand through my greasy hair. Buying time whilst I got my thoughts together. 'Well,' I began, 'someone fired the building, killed Coosie and nearly roasted me into the bargain!'

It was blunt, but in my mind murder and arson ain't the kind of thing that should be prettied up none.

Evans raised an eyebrow and shook his head sadly but stayed quiet.

A soft breeze out of the north was blowing down the canyon. To the west the sky was glowing blood red, stained white with puffy clouds lined with railtrack steel-grey. Evans looked around the ranch again. His eyes were restless, unable to bring them on me.

Finally. 'Weell,' he said, dragging the word out, ready to get official. 'You got any idea who might've…'

'No, I don't rightly know who done it, but one way or another I aim to find out.'

Evans stared at me hard for a moment before saying, 'Where have you been?'

Obviously he knew the answer already because he couldn't fail to notice that our mounts were sweat-slicked and the Leaning

B cattle were back in the corral where they belonged.

'I told you I'd get my cattle back.'

'Hell, Cal! I told you to leave it to the law.'

'An' I told you I'd do it my way from here on in.'

He pushed himself away from the cross poles and pulled himself up to his full height. 'I ain't having this county ripped apart in a ranch feud between you an' Raley!'

'This ain't no feud, John. I took back what was rightly mine.'

'Damn it to hell!' He jabbed a finger at me. 'I done told you the other day they're not legally yourn. Let the court sort it out.'

We both heard the bunkhouse door open. Lantern light threw a weak glow across the ground in the gathering gloom. Slowly the ranch hands began to file out, standing in line behind the town marshal. Evans turned around and eyed the men. He could hardly fail to notice that they were all armed.

'John, the time's come to sort out this trouble,' I began to explain. 'Raley's had the run of this country for far too long and it's about time someone stood up to him.'

'That person being you?' Doc Bay asked. It was the first thing she had said since my arrival.

I turned to her and shrugged. 'If needs be, ma'am,' I said quietly.

'You're a fool, Cal,' she said. 'I had you down for a better man than that. Someone who could work alongside the law. Someone with a strength of character who didn't have to stoop to killing to get what you wanted.'

'Now hold on there, lady! I ain't killed no one, and don't aim to. John knows that I have respect for him and the law. You need to understand that sometimes a body isn't given a choice of which way to jump. Someone has got to stop the rot around here and if it has to be me, then that's just dandy.'

'I'm with you,' Jake Latchford called.

'And me,' Johnny Lowman agreed. And with that there was a chorus of approval from the other men.

Evans stood in the semi-darkness, listening to the unanimous vote of confidence of my words. Doc Bay buried her hands deep into her thick overcoat pockets and stared hard at me. I don't know what she was looking for but I returned the stare because I'd be damned if I was going to be intimidated by a woman over this.

'Cal, I really don't want to say this,' Evans began.

'Well, don't.'

Evans took a deep haul on the cigar and blew out the blue smoke into the air. His coat was buttoned up to the throat, and his badge was pinned on the outside. He pinched the bridge of his nose, then cleared his throat before saying, 'I know you for a fighter, Cal, and one who fights good and fair. I want to tell you that once you step over the mark I can't help you. You're on your own. Humour me and let me sort out the legal side of this cattle matter. You know you can trust me.'

'I can trust *you*,' I laughed bitterly. 'But what about the mayor, and the judge, and the big cattlemen? I don't trust *them*. I need to do this for those men behind you – and for me.'

Evans shook his head wearily. 'If Raley gets a warrant out against you *and* your men for rustling, there'll be nothing I could do to stop him. I'd have to come after you.'

Behind him, a couple of the hands exchanged worried glances. His threat to have them arrested was clearly having the effect he wanted, they were rattled. I knew that one or two of them had warrants against them from other counties and they were using the Leaning B as a short-term haven before riding on. If they caved in to Evans's threat then I'd lose them. But more importantly I'd lose the fight to keep the Leaning B afloat. I had to call John's bluff.

'If you have to do it that way, then I'll say right here and now that it was good knowing you.'

'You mule-headed fool!' Doc Bay gasped. Her normally fair complexion reddened as she stepped up to me. 'Can't you see he's trying to give you a chance to settle things legally? There doesn't have to be gallant knight on a white horse to save the day. Listen to him, please.' She gripped my forearm as she spoke and squeezed hard. I looked deep into her eyes and wanted to hold her close to me.

'Please,' she repeated softly.

No one else moved. Not a soul spoke. The tension was almost visible between Evans, the doc and myself. It was plain that one of us had to give but this time, however, I knew it had to be me. I took Maureen's hand and gently removed it from my sleeve but still held on to it.

'Ma'am, it's late. I'm tired. My crew's dead beat. The day's been long and hard. I figure this ain't the time to be making rash decisions. I'll ride into town come morning and we can talk about this more comfortably then.'

I watched for her reaction. She closed her eyes for a brief moment. The tension seemed to drain away from her face and she smiled. 'I didn't really think you was mule-headed, Cal,' she said. 'Stubborn, mayhaps but not so mule stubborn as not to see good sense.'

Evans stepped in closer, a small sly grin on his rugged face.

'I agree with Maureen, Cal. I think you made a right choice here tonight.'

I nodded. 'Well John, Maureen, I'll see you in the morning, meanwhile there's still work to be done.'

They took my hint to leave and I watched them ride away before turning to the men who were still lined up outside the bunk-house.

Some wore a look of defeat, others were plain disgusted. In one day they had struck back at Raley only to have the law knock the wind out of their sails with the threat of arrest.

I had to give them back their hope, and their pride. I squared up to them and said, 'I want to say thanks. Thanks for your support today in getting back what is rightly ours. And thanks for standing alongside me tonight. Despite what you just heard me say to the doc and the marshal, I ain't through with Raley. Coosie's body is hardly cold in the ground and his death won't be forgotten that easy. But we're goin' to have to change tactics. You've got to trust me and I'll come through for you all. That's all I ask you – trust me.'

'Just like a greenhorn,' Jake spoke up. 'Running off at the mouth an' don't know when to stop.' He laughed, and the others joined him.

They went back into the bunkhouse in high spirits, and I was left standing alone by the corral watching the night stars come out and play in the inky night sky. I filled my pipe with tobacco and drew on the smoke. As far as I could tell, the men hadn't been spooked one bit by Evans's visit. But I knew that they were worried about how Raley might retaliate. Our venture on to his land had been over sixteen hours ago and yet there hadn't been hide nor hair of a vengeful visit from the DR outfit. That worried me more than any lawman's threat. You would have reckoned that any trouble would have been swift and sharp, and so we had steeled ourselves for an attack. Most of the crew had remained near the ranch the day after the raid, armed to the teeth and as jumpy as hell. But nothing happened.

By the second day I had sent Lowman and Swede to scout around O'Fallon Creek whilst the others sat around and waited. The men returned and said that there was nothing out of the ordinary to report. It was as though Raley didn't know it was the Leaning B who had 'stolen' his cattle, but I couldn't really believe that. We had shot at his men, they had returned the fire, and I know that both myself and Hardtack had been recognised by at least a handful of DR men. So the question was: what was the rancher playing at?

Later that night I sat by the corral talking with Jake. We spoke about the situation like two army generals planning a campaign. We knew that the Leaning B wasn't a big outfit like the LO, Diamond Bar or the Mighty XIT. So no one was going to give a damn about a couple of stolen cows from another two-cent outfit. We decided that when we found Coosie's killer, and if we got the chance, we'd handle it our way. Maybe rough up the son of a bitch some, put him through hell and back, then finally send him there.

When that was done we'd leave the country in different directions, Wyoming or Idaho or even over the border to Canada. It would mean leaving the ranch to Christine Dyer and perhaps the men would have to find work elsewhere. But we were still feeling numb and the hollow anger remained over Coosie's death. That, and Raley's ability to side-step the law.

I suppose other men might try and deal with the situation in a different way, but I saw in Jake something of myself. He treasured the sanctity of honour and commitment. It was one of the few things that both he and I knew and had left.

A chilly breeze caressed my face as I stood my horse in a swatch of shadow from a tree, and listened to the chomping sounds from a brace of pronghorn antelopes grazing ahead of us. Hardtack was bent over his horse's neck, fiddling with the bit ring muttering low and soft to keep the animal pacified. It was early morning and we were back up on the Powder Ridge searching for strays that had wandered in our absence. Before riding up here I had told the crew what had been decided, and they seemed happy to let me get on with it.

'You think you're up to it?' Hardtack said suddenly.

'What?'

'I'm askin' if you've got what it takes to carry the fight to Raley and find Coosie's killer, iffen they ain't one and the same?'

I was puzzled by Hardtack's directness. He had been quieter than usual all morning, doubtlessly he had been thinking things over and wanted to get them out into the open.

'I don't know what you think about me,' I replied. 'Of what I'm capable or not capable, but I know one damn thing, and that's once I've given my word on something then I see it through to the end, come what may.'

'You sure?'

'I'm sure.'

'Raley's mighty big around here, Cal.'

'So I keep on hearing.'

'You kill him and there'll be hell to pay.'

I eased myself towards the Texan. 'I tell you this, if I find out he was the one who killed Coosie and tried to kill me, he'll die. No matter what, he'll die.'

Hardtack scratched at his chin stubble for a moment. 'Just who are you?'

'You know as much about me as you need to.'

'Look, goddarn it! Tell me what's happening!'

For the first time I was seeing the Texan in a different light. Up here with me he wasn't as tough as he would like everyone to think he was. He was just another young man in the middle of a difficult situation without the wherewithal to handle it. I honestly felt sorry for him.

'Listen, Hardtack, life is like a woman,' I began. 'One minute she's all loving, and then the next she's tearing your hair out. The one thing you've got to learn is to be able to move with whatever she throws at you. Just like a stalk of corn – it's got to bend in the wind otherwise it'll snap in two.'

'You mean be able to react to anything life throws at you?'

I nodded. 'But make the right moves at the right time. A gambler who throws in his cards at the wrong time might as well become an undertaker. A banker who plays with his customer's money might as well go live with the Hole in the Wall Gang. It's that kind of thing, you know?'

Hardtack nodded and took out his pouch of tobacco, then rolled himself a smoke. I watched the young man as he drew on the quirly and realised how badly shaken up he must have been. I didn't blame him, because it just might have been me if the situation was different. But the way the cards of life had been dealt said it wasn't to be, and I accepted that.

It was youngsters like Hardtack who had my sympathy – they had a reputation to earn and finally to live up to. Not many made it past their twentieth birthday, and a good deal who did ended up bitter and twisted. They were the ones who became infamous as outlaws and killers. I was straight enough in my mind not to let that happen to me.

'What're you thinking about, Cal?'

'Uh? Not too much, Hardtack.'

'You seemed far away.'

'You could say that I've got a load on my mind.'

He smiled. 'I want you to know that what you said has helped me, Cal.'

I dismissed it with a wave of my hand.

'Don't worry about anything,' he said. 'I'll be there guarding your back anytime you need me.'

I smiled and thanked him.

We rode the ridge all morning never coming across one stray. By midday our horses were tired and we were thirsty. We figured that the branding camp was only an hour's ride away so we pointed our mounts that way and started off. We were heading down to a gully when a rifle cracked, and we were showered with stone chippings.

Tag reared up and I had the devil's own to fight him down. My Colt was in my hand before I realised that I had drawn it. Hardtack was looking around to see where the shot came from.

'You hit?' he asked.

'No – you?'

'Not a scratch.'

A second bullet ricocheted only feet in front of Hardtack's head. The sound of the report reverberated across the gulley.

'Damned if I know where it's coming from,' I said.

'We stay here much longer we're going to be hit for sure!'

I agreed. 'We're sitting targets here, let's move out.'

Hardtack's horse leapt forward when the Texan's big rowlers bit into his flanks. I urged Tag on after him and both horses were soon in full flight racing down the gully. But it wasn't out of the hidden gunman's range. He fired off three more shots in quick succession. They were louder than before which meant he was close by but he was no nearer hitting us than before.

We hit the bottom of the gully at a gallop and yanked the horses around the base of the rocks. Up ahead was a jagged defile which could lead us to anywhere. To the left was a jumble of broken boulders. It looked safer than the defile. I shouted to Hardtack to head that way and wheeled Tag around. I checked over my shoulder to see if the Texan was following my lead. As I looked back I saw the tell-tale puff of smoke high up on the ridge where a stone outcrop overlooked us. The sound of the rifle shot followed almost instantly and the bullet buzzed past my head.

We made it amongst the boulders as another shot whanged against rock and skimmed harmlessly away. Both horses were ground hobbled in an instant. I put my pistol away and drew out my rifle.

Hardtack said, 'Life's one big circle of gunplay when you're around, Cal.'

'If it wasn't you'd only get bored. There's got to be some adventure in your life at times,' I replied easily.

'At times! I've hardly paused for breath from last time and you've got me in a shooting match again!'

'Aw, quit belly-aching and put some lead towards that jasper!'

Using the boulders for cover we began to return the sniper's fire. After ten minutes or so I realised that the man's position was perfect for bushwhacking and no amount of shooting from us from behind these rocks was going to make any difference.

'Listen, Hardtack. He's been wily enough to get himself a good shooting place. We're going to have to make a break if we're going to get out of here.'

'You got a plan?'

I nodded. 'He can't hit both of us at the same time, so we've got to run out at the same time but go different ways.'

'That way he won't know which one of us to shoot at first, uh?'

'That's right.'

Hardtack said, 'An' one of us will be able to get away.'

'Both of us – if we're lucky.'

'If he's that bad a shot, you mean.'

'Has he hit us yet?'

Hardtack shook his head.

'He hasn't even hit the horses and they're a bigger target,' I suggested. It was still hard to make the Texan understand so I explained it a little more. 'If he was any kind of a shot we'd be dead meat by now. He hasn't hit us or the horses which means…'

'He doesn't want to kill us,' he realised at last.

'Yeah.'

'So why don't we just get up and walk out of here?'

I sighed heavily. 'He might not want to kill us but being shot any place ain't that much fun.'

He nodded slowly. God, he was making it hard work. It was like talking to a five-year-old kid. 'OK, then. On my count of three, you run over to your left and I go to the right. After that we'll work our way back up the ridge and see if we can get our hands on whoever it is up there.'

'Sure.'

'You ready? OK then, one … two … *three!*'

SEVEN

Although I knew Hardtack wasn't too pleased with my plan, there was no way he was going to be left out of the action. And with boyish enthusiasm he raced away from the boulder and let rip with a mighty yell. I guess it could have been one of those famous rebel yells, but never having heard one I couldn't rightly say it was so. But what it managed to do was confuse the hidden sniper so much that he didn't even have the chance to let off one shot at either of us. Unharmed we both made it safely to the next area of cover.

Now we had the task of climbing our way up the gully, and get our hands on our would-be assassin before he shot us. I had to holster my revolver and use both hands to begin the ascent. It was going to be hard as my hands had hardly healed from being burnt. So I ignored the pain of cutting stones as I slowly started my way up the rockface.

Half-way up several blisters ripped open and began to bleed. I rested on the first ledge I reached, and keeping my back to the wall, ripped my bandanna in two. My lips were cracked and dry but sweat ran freely down my back and face, plastering my shirt against my sweating body. I tightly bound my hands, leaving the fingers free and continued on my way. Several times I looked for Hardtack but couldn't spot the Texan. I just prayed to God that he didn't reach the assassin first and try something stupid before I got there. That would have been just like him to try and do something heroic, just to make him look good in my eyes. The damn fool kid would probably get himself shot!

I physically jumped when the rifle opened up again, and steeled myself for the impact which never came. It sounded close, and I pushed myself on with more urgency. A couple of more minutes would see me to the top.

I was almost there when the high crack of a handgun was quickly followed by the answering boom of the rifle. All I could think of was that Hardtack had beaten me to the top, and was now exchanging shots with the gunman without waiting for me. More shots from both weapons were fired, and I finally hauled myself over the ridge and lay flat on my stomach drawing in great gulps of air.

About fifteen feet away, hidden behind a boulder, was the mysterious rifleman. He was using an old Burnside Spencer carbine, the short-barrelled type they used to issue to the cavalry. For some reason he was older than I expected, and wore a long, straggly beard shot through with grey. A slouch hat shaded his eyes from the sun and his clothes had seen better days. Obviously he hadn't seen or sensed I was there because he concentrated on laying down more lead to where Hardtack was hidden behind a boulder.

Slowly I got to my feet drawing out my

pistol at the same time. My intention was to get as close as I could, and get the drop on him but he must have realised that he was in danger, and spun around to face me. The Spencer boomed out its .50 calibre death and I hit the ground with a bone-jarring thud.

I could feel the pain in my right foot, shooting up my leg like a forest-fire. Suddenly my head spun, and my vision became blurred. But apart from that I was still breathing and alive. I tried to focus on the gunman but kept seeing two ghostly figures of him dancing back and forth in my eyeline. Any chance of shooting *and* hitting him was out of the question. I had to leave that to Hardtack.

But then the gunman suddenly turned and ran down the blind side of the gully without firing another shot. Perhaps he thought he had killed me and I wasn't about to disillusion him. I heard a horse whinny and then the sound of hooves striking hard ground at the gallop. He was getting away and there was nothing I could damn well do about it.

'Cal!' Hardtack's voice echoed in my ears. 'Cal! Where the goddarn hell are you?'

'Here, Hardtack! Over here.'

The Texan suddenly loomed over me. 'You hit?'

'My foot. I think he shot my foot.'

Hardtack bent down and took each foot, examining them in turn. 'Hell, boy! He just shot off one of your heels is all!'

I propped myself up on my elbows and looked down at my feet. By God he was right. That jasper had shot off one of my boot heels! I must have taken a whack on the head when I was knocked down. Hardtack held out a hand, I took it and he helped me up on to my feet. After a moment or two of dizziness I shook my leg around a bit to get the blood going again, I felt better.

'C'mon, Cal. He's getting away,' Hardtack enthused.

I shook my head. 'By the time we get our horses he'll be long gone.'

'Couldn't we track him?'

I indicated the stony ground. 'Not over this stuff. Not by me anyway.'

He spat out a curse and looked over the edge of the gulley at the gunman's dust cloud, and shook his head sadly. I knew that if Hardtack couldn't track him, then I'd have no better chance.

'I wonder who hired him?' I thought aloud.

'What makes you figger someone did?'

'Think about it, Hardtack. Why would someone want us killed, or out of the way? What have we done to anyone in this part of the country to hurt them?'

'You're thinking 'bout Raley, again?'

'I wouldn't put it past him.'

Hardtack looked out across the land, watching a bird riding high on the thermals before saying, 'Seems everything keeps coming back to him, don't it?'

I nodded but said nothing.

He said, 'Why don't we go pay him a visit, and get this thing sorted out the oncet?'

I weighed up the question in my mind before answering. 'Well, firstly, we don't know if it is Raley who's behind all this and secondly, if someone does face him, it will be me not *us*, Hardtack.'

'I'm as much part of this ranch as you are, Cal. So I got an interest in what happens.'

'I ain't denying that. But I don't want you facing down Raley with no good reason.'

'No good reason! No good reason! You call being shot at no good reason?'

I held my hands up to pacify the Texan who had become red-faced with anger. 'Hold up, Hardtack. Now listen to me, will you? I want you to understand one thing – if Raley is the man behind all this, then I'll deal with him. I don't want anyone else getting hurt. Do you understand me?'

The big Texan nodded petulantly. I repeated myself to make it absolutely clear to the Texan, 'I don't want to have anyone else getting hurt or killed over this, do you hear me? I still owe it to Brecker to see this through, and I aim to do just that. And I don't want a greenhorn gunhand getting in my way.'

The youngster's face had altered – hardened and become thin-lipped. I could see my words were hurting him but there was no way I wanted to see him killed. Especially so after losing Coosie not so long ago.

'What we need to do now is get to the branding camp and get on with ranching. You with me?'

'Yeah,' he said reluctantly.

The remainder of our ride was made in silence. I knew that the Texan's pride had been damaged but I had to be uncharitable to keep the boy alive. If he wanted to sulk then that was OK by me, it saved him from being killed needlessly. Though what he said was true, it was time to get things sorted out with Raley once and for all. Although the big face-to-face showdown that Hardtack had in mind wasn't the way I wanted it. And to tell you the truth, I don't rightly know the right way.

The branding camp was a welcome sight. And the smell of good strong coffee was a pleasure to the senses. Hardtack and me rode over to the corral, off-saddled and rubbed down the horses, leaving them to eat and drink their fill. They certainly had earned it. As soon as the horses had been seen to we turned towards the camp-fire and helped ourselves to the coffee.

Swede came over and asked Hardtack what we had been up to but the tone of his reply stopped the cowboy from asking him anything else. Swede sauntered back to stoking the branding fire, muttering something about close-mouthed Texans and a sheep's backside. I'm glad that he said that out of Hardtack's earshot because the Texan would have knocked him out. Thankful to get off my feet for a spell, I dropped to the floor and rested my back up against a small boulder with my feet stuck out in front of me. I began the coffee as I watched the men work. I must have dozed off for a while because when I awoke Hardtack was arguing with Jake.

'The hell I will!'

'You'll do as you're told!' Latchford said.

Hardtack vigorously shook his head. 'I

ain't gonna do it, I tell you!'

Latchford dropped the branding iron back into the fire and stepped in closer to Hardtack. His voice was cold as the winter's wind. 'I told you to take them calves back, and that's what you're gonna do.'

'I don't have to if I don't want to,' came the Texan's choleric reply.

Grudgingly I got to my feet and stood alongside a couple of the hands who were watching the heated exchange. They gave me sideways glances to see if I was going to interrupt but I kept my mouth shut. This was between the ramrod and a cowboy, and they didn't need me poking my nose in where it didn't belong.

'Them calves don't belong to us, Hardtack. You'll return them to our neighbour, and right now.'

'Neighbour!' he spat. 'The DR spread ain't our neighbours. I call 'em liars, cheats and cold-blooded killers!'

There was a murmur of agreement from some of the cowboys. Jake Latchford took a deep breath and held it a second or two. He was being patient with the Texan. Slowly he said, 'You don't take anything from your neighbours, you know that. So why don't you just do as you're told?'

Hardtack looked over, and jerked his chin towards me. 'What have you got to say about all this?'

Latchford turned to look at me. I couldn't read any expression in his face at all. So I said that I agreed with Jake. The Texan and the ramrod turned and faced each other again. Around them the noise of the camp filled the air, other hands were oblivious to the scene as they carried on working, and the cattle were ignorant of the trouble they were causing. The men locked stares for a while, and it was Hardtack who finally broke it.

'I'll do it,' he said. 'But when I get back there'll be some changes, I'm warning you.' He turned and strode off towards the corral.

Jake Latchford looked at me, and gave a curt nod of his head.

Twenty-four hours had almost passed since Hardtack had ridden off pushing those few calves to the DR spread, and still the Texan hadn't reappeared. By my estimate the journey shouldn't have taken him more than ten hours but after the incident with the sniper I was fearful for the young man's life. I began to think what if the sniper decided to try his luck once again and seeing a lone, helpless rider decide to finish off what he had started? The very thought made me shudder. On the other hand he may have chosen to run out on us, but I hoped I knew Hardtack, and I felt that he wouldn't do that to his friends.

I called Chet Mills over, and told him to saddle up a couple of good mounts and load up some supplies. I had a nagging notion in the back of my head that something was not quite right. There was still four or five hours of good light left when we rode out of the Leaning B corral and headed off towards the branding canyon. We made good time because there was no need to do any tracking. That was in our favour because the ground around the canyon and the surrounding area was a patchwork of hoofmarks.

'You know the land better than me, Chet,' I said. 'What route would Hardtack have taken?'

Mills stabbed a finger towards the gently folding land north-west of the canyon. 'He's pushing young calves … he'll take the easy route.'

'Then we'll head that way, too.'

We rode hard for a couple of hours before picking up a likely trail. It appeared that he was in no great hurry; letting the calves stray a bit, then chousing them together before moving on. I felt a little easier now we had a trail to follow.

Chet Mills said, ''Pears that Hardtack is aimin' to come in round the north end of the DR spread, by way of the ridge and then move west to the ranch house.'

'If he means to take them all the way.'

'Yeah, I suppose he could let them little 'uns loose to find their own way home once he gets on DR land.'

161

'If he did that,' I said slowly, thinking about it, 'then he should've been in the bunkhouse hours ago.'

Mills nodded, then shrugged. We pushed on further.

A persistent wind was picking up. It blew down from the top of the Powder Ridge bringing a chill that bit into our exposed flesh. My cord jacket was warm enough to keep out the wind but even with the collar turned up it wouldn't be adequate for a night in the open.

There were only a few good hours of sunlight left to carry on the search with, and I was thinking about turning back when we topped a gully and saw Hardtack. He was at the bottom trapped beneath his horse. We reached him pretty quickly but the boy was out to the world. Chet wetted his neckerchief and wiped it around the Texan's mouth. He did it once more before Hardtack started to come around.

He opened his swollen eyes slowly and looked at the both of us before saying,

'Jesus, boys. Am I rightly glad to see you.'

His horse had been shot from under him in the neck. The blood had dried black around the entry holes, and the blow flies hungrily ate their meal with an annoyingly gleeful buzzing. I slapped them away with my hat but they soon came back.

Hardtack's face was ashen, his cheeks were sunken and his dark-circled eyes were filled with pain. He was at that stage where any hurt was no more annoying than the buzzing of those flies. If his leg had been trapped for any length of time, then I knew for a fact that he was going to lose it. I'd seen it in a mining camp a time before when a tunnel had collapsed and a miner had gotten himself trapped beneath the rock fall. We couldn't get to him for three hours – it proved long enough for him to lose both legs from gangrene.

'You hurting, boy?' I asked.

He lazily shook his head. 'Can't feel my leg any more, Cal. My ribs feel like they're on fire.'

Mills shot me a sad-faced glance, one that said that the Texan was all done cowboying.

I cleared my throat. 'Listen, Hardtack. We're gonna haul your horse off you. Maybe it'll hurt like hell but we gotta get you out from under it.'

'Don't worry me none, Cal. I can't feel my leg no more.'

I reached in my saddlebag and brought out a pint bottle of whiskey. I pulled the stopper and squatting down offered it to the Texan. 'Here, son,' I said. 'Take a good pull on this. It won't stop the pain but it'll deaden it some.'

Hardtack sucked greedily on the bottle before letting go with a long sigh.

'That was worth waiting for,' he said.

'You keep with that, Hardtack, whilst me and Chet fix ropes around this horse meat.'

'My pleasure,' he answered smiling.

The Texan was certainly putting up an act of bravado and I wasn't going to deny him this. Mills and myself worked quickly to tie the ropes around the blue roan's neck and hindquarters, then dallied the ends around our saddlehorns. Mills took the reins to our horses, and on my signal, slowly began walking them forward.

The dead weight of the roan began lifting off of Hardtack's trapped leg, and I got a good hold of him under his armpits. Once the animal was shifted high enough I pulled Hardtack out. He hardly made a whimper as his body was hauled free of the dead weight. I laid him down gently on the hard ground, and looked up at Mills approaching us with a big-bladed Bowie knife in his hand.

He said, 'We'd best see to that leg of his. It ain't gonna be a pretty sight.'

Mills unbuckled the Texan's woolly chaps and removed them. He cut away the pants' leg, and laid it open. He was right about the sight. The exposed skin was already in a gangrenous state; colours ran from black to yellow, purple to blue and back gain. The smell was evil.

Hardtack sank the last of the whiskey and slurred, 'Ain't good news, is it boys? I won't be dancing at the next fandango, that's for sure.'

A cold wind stroked my face with its icy fingers and I shivered. 'No, son. Reckon not.'

'Don't worry, Cal. Couldn't dance worth shit, anyhows.'

I laughed emptily. 'Listen, Hardtack. Can you remember what happened here?'

'By God, yes. I was bushwhacked by a couple of gunmen. They shot my horse from under me first, and when they saw I was trapped they rode off with them goddarn calves laughing so much you could've heard 'em in Burdick County!'

'You see their faces?' Mills asked.

'No. They wore flour sack masks.'

I began to untie the ropes to give me some time to think.

'They didn't head for the DR spread!' Hardtack said as though he could read my mind. 'I stayed conscious long enough to see them ride toward the north end of the ridge.'

Mills knelt down with a small sack in his hand and he dug in a hand. He brought out a tin of bear grease and a couple of rolls of bandages.

He said, 'Here, Hardtack. I'm going to see to them ribs before we set out for the ranch.'

'Too late for that, Chet.'

'Aw quit belly-aching. Let me get on with what I know about, OK?'

Hardtack was in no shape to argue and allowed Mills to get on with his doctoring. I finished coiling my rope and tied it back on the saddle. I told them that I was going after the bushwhackers and that Mills should get Hardtack back to the Leaning B as quickly as possible. I threw him my spare quart of whiskey. Mills was surprised but accepted it without a word.

I pulled the little quarterhorse around, and headed out to where Hardtack had shown me where the attack came from. It didn't take much to find out where they had lain in wait; there were a lot of boot prints, cigarette butts and discarded cartridge jackets. I picked one of them up and rolled it in my fingers, examining it. I didn't recognise the calibre but judging from the wounds in the roan's neck it must've been a heavy one, maybe a .45/47 or even a .50. I pocketed the shell for later. The tracks headed towards the Powder River Ridge and the eastern section of the DR range and I set off following them.

The tall ponderosa pines cast their dark shadows over the land as I approached the base of the ridge. The bushwhackers had left a trail that was easy enough to follow. Obviously they had thought that time was on their side; even stopping to butcher one of the calves. Apart from hacking out a couple of goodly sized steaks, the carcass was left whole.

As I slowly rode past the calf I got the feeling that someone was watching me. I searched the top of the ridge but there was no one skylighted – only an idiot would have been that foolish. And looking into the trees I could only guess that someone might be lurking in the black shadows or behind the grey boulders.

I transferred the reins into my left hand and let my right drift to the reassuring weight of the .45 on my hip. The tension was building up in my chest like a tight band, and I was sure that trouble was lurking around ready to strike. Throughout the whole affair I was pleased with myself that I had not aimed my gun to kill anyone. In the whole of my life I can readily admit to killing three men. But I was a paid lawman then, and each time had been in self-defence. I'll allow that I've used a gun to threaten many a man but there's a fine line you tread when you actually go ahead and pull the trigger. The question I've always asked myself is: do you do it because there's a need or because you've done it before and it is the easiest way out? That's how I think many of the so-called gunfighters start out. They reached the stage where killing a man means nothing, and they actually began to like it.

I don't know if I'd kill those who had crippled Hardtack, and that's the God's honest truth. The Texan was going to be good for nothing; just another one-legged hobo working in a store or bar because he's pitied. Me, I'd rather die if I couldn't ride a horse, and *that's* the truth.

The tracks leading into the pines had been clear but now it looked like the riders had split up. One set of prints led off into the trees whilst the others out to the west, and in the direction of the DR spread. As I sat nervously in the saddle I was conscious to the fact that I might be a sitting target. The feeling of being watched was still with me. Around me the shadows grew deeper and the colour was beginning to drain out of the sky. I had less than an hour to find one of the gunmen but first I had to make up my mind which way to go.

The wind shifted and blew in my face, and carried on it was the smell of cooking meat. I smiled at the sky. Either the gunman was so sure that he hadn't been followed or was setting a trap. I figured for the former and chose to enter the pines.

My little quarter-horse shied from entering the dark trees, he was more accustomed to being around noisy cattle than the eerie forest silence, but I persuaded him to go on. Once amongst the trees the heavy scent of pine needles filled the air, and the closeness of the branches slowed us down to a walk. Now and then the smell of food reached me and the horse. He snorted, shook his head and chomped on the bit. Maybe he, like me, was hungry too.

The going got harder as we started up the ridge following what must have been an animal trail. Night was almost upon us when we broke out of the treeline and out on to the ridge proper. I had lost the scent of the food a while back, and relied more on my sense of direction to keep going on the right track. Thankfully I wasn't let down but if it wasn't for that little horse shying as we attempted to pass a weather-slicked overhanging rock, I might have missed the entrance to the cave.

The fissure in the rock face was just big enough for a man and pony to squeeze through. I decided to leave the horse ground-hobbled outside, and drawing out my single-action .45, went inside. It wasn't totally dark but I still had to feel my way along the rock as the path dipped down a little before opening out into a big cavern.

A small cooking fire had died down to the embers and gave out a feeble glow. It was obvious whoever stayed here was a regular visitor for there was a supply of airtights stacked on a rocky ledge, some buffalo hides were heaped to one side and there was a cot bed made out of pine logs.

I made a more thorough search to make sure no one was hiding in the deep shadows. I decided to bring the little quarter horse in and wait for the mystery man to return. Most of the light had gone now and an indigo sky had replaced it. It wouldn't be long till it was totally dark, so I guessed that my wait wouldn't be that long.

Once I had fetched the horse I found out where the supply of oats and water was, and took care of the animal. I didn't loosen his cinch just in case I needed to get out of there quickly. For myself I found a tin of oysters and tucked into them. When I sat next to the fire, feeding it with small twigs and branches, I saw a lump of beef which had fallen into the embers and was almost charcoaled now. If it hadn't been for the man being so careless I wouldn't have found his hideaway. Taking one of the hides from the cot, I covered my shoulders and settled down to wait for his return.

The man had great confidence that his hiding place would remain a secret because he approached it as if he hadn't a worry under the skies. His voice was loud enough to carry for miles as he gave a slurred, out-of-tune rendition of 'Forty miles a day on beans and hay'. That gave me the idea that he was an ex-frontier cavalryman.

Throwing off the hide I moved into the darkness of the rear of the cave bringing my horse with me, using my neckerchief to muzzle him. I watched silently as the man entered the cave, and staggered over to the fire. The ex-cavalryman threw twigs and thicker logs on to the fire, then fanned the embers with his hat. It soon sprung into life and lit up the cave a little more. He stood watching the flames leap and crackle, swaying on his feet a bit, before pulling a bottle from his pocket and taking a healthy gulp from it.

All the while I was waiting for him to turn around so I could see his face. From his build I had him down as the sniper but I wanted to be sure. I stepped away from the horse and began to walk towards him. He must have sensed my presence for I was no more than ten feet from him when he spun around and faced me. Either out of shock or surprise he dropped the bottle. By sheer luck it didn't break.

My stomach gave a lurch as I recognised him as the sniper. Then everything I had thought I would do disappeared under a cloud of overwhelming anger, and I launched myself at him.

He was totally unprepared for my attack

and my first blow caught him in the stomach that doubled him up. I grabbed a handful of hair and pulled him up so we were face-to-face. Spittle ran out of his mouth into his dark golden beard. His eyes held a mixture of pain and anger. I hit him with a clubbing right which broke his nose, and made my knuckle pop. He fell to the ground, and I was left holding a fistful of greasy hair.

In the red glow of the fire his blood appeared black as it ran out of his nose and into his moustache. Shaking his head like an animal would do, he struggled to get back onto his feet. I allowed him to get half-way up before kicking him in the stomach. He hit the ground face-first.

I waited until he rolled over on to his back before saying, 'Did you ambush that rider?'

He spat out a gooey mixture of blood and spittle for an answer.

I kicked him in the ribs.

'Who paid you to shoot at us?'

'You son … of … a … bitch,' he said painfully.

I kicked him some more.

'Was it Raley?' Another kick. 'Tell me you sorry bastard, was it Raley?'

He gasped with every kick as it landed, then finally said, 'No more... I'll tell you...' He fought hard for his breath. 'Don't be kicking me any more.' His breathing was ragged and he began to take quick, small breaths. 'My chest ... hurts...!'

He grabbed at the front of his buckskins, pulling at them, trying to tear them off. 'Oh, sweet Jesus, it hurts!'

Even in the feeble glow of firelight his face was as white as a sheet. Suddenly his head jerked back like he'd been punched by an invisible fist. His body juddered, then he was still. I bent over him, cautious that he might be playing at being dead ready to drive a knife into my guts, and kept one hand on the grips of my revolver.

'C'mon, get up. I ain't done with you yet.' I dug him with the point of my boot, but he lay there unmoving. 'Quit tryin' to fool me, oldster. It ain't workin'.'

Finally I knelt down beside him and placed my free hand on his chest. I couldn't feel a heartbeat nor see his chest heaving up and down. The damn old fool had gone and died on me. His heart had given out before letting on what he knew! I cursed my own stupid anger, in allowing it to get the better of me. Now I was no better off than before, and any chance of discovering who it was trying to get me out of the way had disappeared.

Daybreak couldn't have come any sooner. I hadn't managed to get a full hour's worth of sleep all night. My conscience hadn't allowed me the luxury of sleep; keeping the old-cavalryman's face in my head all the while. Sometime in the early hours of the morning I gave up trying and sat at the mouth of the cave wrapped in a blanket and puffed on my corn pipe.

The eerie light of the false dawn speckled the tree tops and stone face alike. Shadows scampered back from where they had come from and when the sun appeared it brought out the daytime creatures. I sat there watching the land come alive before I knocked out the dead ashes from my pipe. I fetched out my horse and belongings from the cave. Whilst I was in there, and out of respect to the ex-frontier cavalryman, I covered him with his blanket and muttered a few words of apology. His carbine was still tied to the saddle and I removed it to get a better look in the daylight.

As I held it in my shaking hands, rolling it over and examining it, there was no doubt that it was a Burnside Spencer. With the breechblock lowered my guess that it was of the .50 calibre variety was confirmed. The old man had kept the weapon in prime condition. The wooden stock still gleamed, the barrel was hardly pitted and the mechanism worked sweetly. Not bad for a weapon almost fifteen years old. I figured that there could only be a handful of men this side of the Powder River who owned such a carbine, so it shouldn't prove too hard to find a name for its owner.

As the sun grew stronger I finally swung

up into the saddle and headed back to the Leaning B. Leaving the old man behind was perhaps the best I could do for him. He'd probably lived a lonely life with only his horse for company so it figured out better this way.

I made one stop off for water and a chew on some jerked beef I had taken from the cave and then I headed for the ranch. Some miles away I suddenly changed my mind and headed towards town. I guessed that Hardtack would be in the safe hands of Doc Bay by now and I needed to know if everything was OK with him. Well, that and the chance of seeing her again.

I rode into town about meal-time, so my stomach told me. I headed for Joe's Café and downed two cups of coffee before ordering my food. When the eggs, steak and potatoes were inside me I felt much better. Ready enough to go over to the doc's and find out how Hardtack was.

Out in the street it was the first time that I noticed that there were buntings and banners strung up across the buildings, flapping in the wind. A man dressed up as a clown was putting handbills on the upright post outside the barbers.

THE CIRCUS IS HERE!

Youngsters swarmed around him like bees to a honey pot and he put up with all their questions, tugging and pulling with the good humour any clown should possess. They tagged along with him as he went to the dry goods store and put up a second poster. This one read:

TONIGHT IN THE CIRCUS:
COME AND SEE WILD ANIMALS!
THRILL AT
MYSTERIOUS MARVELS!
GASP AT AMAZING FEATS
OF STRENGTH!
SHOW BEGINS AT NIGHTFALL.

I felt happy as I turned away and went back

into the doctor's place.

But I was unprepared for the sight that greeted me, Hardtack was propped up in bed with the upper half of his body swathed in bandages. His face was ashen and shone like a mare's well-groomed coat. Dark half-circles under his eyes made him look cadaverous. He was asleep and every breath he drew sounded painful, rasping out of his throat like a rusty saw.

Maureen tugged at my arm, pulling me away from the cowboy and led me back into her parlour.

'He's very sick, Cal,' she said.

I swallowed hard and nodded.

'He may not pull through.'

'Hell! 'Course he will, he's Texan!'

Maureen slowly shook her head. 'He's busted up real bad inside, and I'm going to operate on his leg tomorrow.'

'You mean you can save it?'

'Uh-uh. It's got to come off – the poison's spreading. If I don't…'

'Yeah, I know. You don't have to tell me.'

Secretly I was frightened of the very thought of having any part of my body chopped off. And the look on Maureen's face said that she knew that. I sat down heavily in the chair and scrubbed a hand over my face. Maureen laid her hand gently on my shoulder and rubbed it lightly. Her voice was soft as velvet when she spoke.

'I really don't think that he'll make it, Cal. He may be a big, tough Texan but gangrene doesn't respect anyone. Even if I take his leg off and he lives, what good would he be as a cowboy? How many ranchers would hire him?'

'I would.'

She smiled reassuringly. 'I know you would, Cal. But others wouldn't.'

'There don't have to be any others, Maureen.'

'I don't think there's enough round these parts to hold a man like you down for too long, Cal.'

I looked up at her. She was looking out of the window with a far-away expression on her face. I turned my face away before she could look back. 'Ma'am,' I stood up. 'Maureen, right at this moment I don't know what I'll be doing in a week or a month's time. But I do know that someone has to pay for what they did to Hardtack, Coosie and what they're trying to do to the Leaning B. I gave my word to them men that I'd do everything I can to help them, and I aim to stick to it.'

'No doubt you will.'

'I know that this might be a hard thing for you to do, Maureen. If Hardtack is going to die – let him die in one piece. Let him go with some dignity. What d'you say?'

She thought about that for a moment, then nodded. 'If he's agreeable, then I reckon he can die with respect.'

'Thank you, Maureen. Thank you.'

'But what about after that? After all this trouble is over, what then?'

I shrugged my shoulders, I didn't have an answer to that.

She said, 'Will you simply saddle up and go? The lonesome rider moving on again?'

The words caught in her throat, she was very close to tears.

I moved closer to her holding out my hand. She took it and I pulled her close. I could feel her trembling against me and as we stood there embracing I realised one of the reasons why I stayed was right here in this room. When we kissed it seemed the most natural thing in the world to do. When we broke away our faces were still close.

'Cal, I'm not used…' she began.

'It's OK, Maureen. Nor am I.'

My attempt at being amusing didn't work. She broke away and stood by the mantelpiece with her back to me. Speaking quietly, almost in a whisper, she said, 'I don't know where this is going to lead us. I wasn't ready for this to happen.'

The faint spark of a relationship was dying. I couldn't let it go out. 'I don't know what to say, Maureen. It wasn't like I planned any of this.'

She turned to face me, and moved in close, her hand riding up and down my arm.

'I know that, Cal. It's just … just that my feelings towards you are strong but I don't know how you feel towards me.'

'Well, ma'am. I know that I'm fond of you. Real fond. And, uh … I've taken a shine to you since we first met. And, em, well, since we both like each other, let's make it official.' I stood there running the brim of my hat through my hands, then scratched my head as I gave my impromptu speech waiting for an answer.

'You asking to be my beau?'

I stupidly nodded my reply.

'Why thank you, Will Calhoun. I'd be happy to have you escort me to the circus tonight.'

'Tonight?'

'Well, sure. Had you forgotten?'

'No, no. I hadn't planned on anything…'

She laughed. 'Poor old Cal.' She ran her fingers gently across my face. 'You should bring all the boys out, and let them let their hair down. There's going to be a fandango over at Parson's yard after the circus. It would give you a chance for a well-earned break, as well.'

That was one thing with which I couldn't disagree. It would do the boys good to have some fun for a change.

EIGHT

The next thing I did was have my first real bath in a long while. I used the Chinese place just down the street to the surgery. On the way there I stopped off at the ostlers and gave the young help there a dollar to ride out to the Leaning B with a message for Jake to bring the boys into town for a fun night out.

For the rest of the day I walked around town. Around three I went over to a saloon near the cattle pens, bought a beer, and helped myself to a pickled egg. I washed the dryness of the egg down with the beer and then ordered a whiskey. I took the drink over to a table near the window and looked out at the street.

Over at the dry goods store I watched a man as he loaded a flatbed wagon with sacks whilst his young son arranged them, struggling under the heavy weight but not complaining. A group of women, all wearing large brimmed hats and carrying parasols, were talking earnestly as they passed. Two drunken cowboys were trying to navigate their way across the street without being knocked down by horsemen or wagons. One stumbled and fell on his back; his soused partner bent down to help but fell down as well. The two of them stayed in the middle of the street; one laughing, the other snoring, all traffic missing them.

I'd also gone to the barbers for a trim and a shave, then bought myself a new outfit to replace the borrowed clothes. I felt good in blue jeans, dark-navy cotton range shirt and I had treated myself to a pair of boots with fancy stitching made by the Justin Boot company of Fort Worth, Texas. I got my pipe going and decided to give it a few more minutes before I went over to Maureen's to check on Hardtack. I was just getting up when Johnny Evans walked in. He still carried the scattergun.

He smiled widely when he saw me and changed direction to come over.

'Hiddy, Cal,' he said, putting out a hand as he approached. I shook it and slapped him on the back.

'How's it goin', John?'

Evans pulled one of the chairs away from the table, turned it around backwards and straddled it. Just like one of the boys. He put the shotgun down on the tabletop and pushed his hat further back on his head. Today he was wearing a red and white shirt with a large blue neckerchief that hung down to his belly. Over this he wore a tan leather jacket with brass buttons and had fringes hanging down from the shoulders. His badge was pinned on the breast pocket.

I said, 'You got news on them cattle?'

'Don't beat about the brush, Cal! Hell, just say what's on your mind!'

'I ain't thinking this is funny.'

'No, it ain't.'

I got up and went to the bar, bought a couple of beers and gave one to the lawman.

I stayed standing. Then I asked him a second time.

'Hey. Calm down a mite, Cal. I was looking for you. Maureen told me you was in town and what happened to that Texan. Did you find out who done it?'

I thought about mentioning the ex-cavalry man but then decided against it. I shook my head. I was looking out of the window at the people moving along. 'So, anyway,' I said, not wanting to let Evans get side-tracked.

'Oh, sure. Well, I went out and saw that Weatherly feller, the vet, yesterday. He says that what was done, all the paperwork, the examinations, was all legal.'

He wasn't telling me anything new. 'How the hell did he manage that?'

Evans shrugged his shoulders, then took a mouthful of beer. He wiped away his froth moustache with the back of his hand. 'Don't matter none anyhows.'

I turned away from the window. I thought I could see an evil flame flicker deep in his eyes.

'He's dead,' Evans supplied.

Now why wasn't I surprised? 'What happened to him?'

'My deputy found him this afternoon. Said it was one of the damnedest things he'd ever seen.'

'What? What did he see?'

'They found Weatherly's body about a half-mile out of town.'

'Had he been shot, stabbed or what?'

'You're not following me. His body was found out of town but his head was caught up on the cowcatcher of the noon-day train.'

'Sweet Jesus!'

'He must've fallen on the tracks, and the train came along and chop!' He made a knife's edge with one hand and slapped it into the palm of the other. 'Strange thing is though, no one knows what he was doing out that way. There's no one lives out there and his horse was stabled. Though his clothes did reek of beer.'

'So what happens now?'

'Now? I don't follow you.'

'The cattle?'

Evans shut his eyes for a second or two before saying, 'They're still Raley's property. It's all legal.'

'Goddammit to hell!'

The lawman put out a hand to pacify me. 'Now don't go getting mad again, Cal. I told you I'd try and sort everything out but there just ain't no more I can do.'

'Let me put it this way, John,' I said. 'From here on in you don't have to worry yourself.'

'Meaning?'

'Meanin', I've had it with Raley and them cows.'

Evans stared at me and said, 'I did all I could for you and the ranch, Cal.'

I nodded yes.

Evans hauled himself out of the chair and stood up. He picked up his scattergun and held it casually in his hand. I was back looking out of the window and when I turned he was gone.

Walking over to Maureen's I'd made up my mind to tell everything to her and Hardtack.

As I crossed the street two of his deputies were nailing up a sign on a post outside the Longhorn saloon. It was an ordnance saying that if anyone should try and kill the circus tiger for fun, they would be fined $1,000 and run out of town. I'd heard tales that some hunters killed the animal just to make fancy belts out of their hide. Snakeskin belts, yeah. But tiger belts?

The doc was seeing to a patient and waved me through to the back room where Hardtack was. I knocked softly before pushing the door open, steeling myself for whatever sight might greet me. The room smelled of death. Hardtack was awake but didn't look any better. The bedsheets were drawn up to his throat and his face was even whiter. His eyes seemed to have sunk deeper into his skull, peering dull and lifeless out of dark sockets. He managed a weak smile and I returned a hearty one.

'Hiya, Hardtack.'

'Lo, Cal.'

I pulled up a chair and straddled it. 'I

think I've got some good news for you.'

'God knows I need it.'

I nodded yes. I looked around the room for some water, or anything to drink. There was nothing about so I took out a half-pint of bourbon I'd bought earlier. There were no glasses either so I uncorked it and offered Hardtack the first drop.

He wasn't the kind of man who'd refuse and I waited for a turn at the bottle.

After we finished a couple of pulls each he said, 'What's the good news, then?'

I started with the sniper, and how I tracked him to the cave and eventually killed him. Hardback sucked on the bottle whilst he heard me out.

'Why did he do it?' he asked.

'That's something we're never going to find out. Damn it! Every which way I turn comes into a dead canyon.'

'You ain't gonna quit, are you?' I heard the desperation in his voice.

'I sure feel like it right now. Ain't nothing gone right since I signed on for Brecker and the Leaning B. To tell you the truth, Hardtack, once this whole mess is cleared up I reckon on quitting. Sell out to Dyer, give Jake most of the money and move on.'

The Texan looked at me for a moment, appearing like he didn't know me or what I was talking about. He took another mouthful of bourbon. He said, 'I don't give a damn about the way you feel! You made a promise to bring in Coosie's killer and keep the Leaning B from going under. Now you're making noises like some goddamn female!'

The venom in his words seemed to sap the strength out of him and he lay back on his pillows with his eyes closed. I couldn't blame him for his outburst, and maybe it did seem like I was whining, but I wanted to let someone know how I felt. A minute or two passed before Hardback reopened his eyes.

I said, 'Look, I think I'd better explain a couple of more things to you, Hardtack. I've done a whole lot of thinking about the business with them cows Raley's managed to get hold of.'

'I'm listenin'.'

'He had to know that Brecker's cows were good breeding stock, right? Up until that time Brecker had been managing to keep the Leaning B going. So what happened to make Raley think he could step in and frighten the kid off?'

Hardtack thought on that for a moment. 'I can't rightly say.'

'Was there some kind of dispute between the two of them before?'

Hardtack shook his head. 'Not that I know.'

'The way I see it is that there was something between Raley and Brecker that made them hate each other. I know that John was scared of Raley but still he had the spunk to face him in a town full of people he thought despised him.'

'All except Chrissie Dyer.'

I took the bottle from the Texan and drank. Then said, 'Yeah, all except her. Perhaps she's the key to all this. Was there anything between her and Raley before Billy Joe appeared?'

Hardtack shifted his weight in the bed, setting himself more upright. I helped by puffing up the pillows behind his back. The effort weakened him a bit and I waited for his answer.

'All I know is that she had been seeing other men before Brecker made serious advances,' he said. 'Billy Joe liked her the first time he clapped eyes on her but she was cold and distant to him.'

Suddenly I remembered Coosie's outburst about her when we were breakfasting a while back. I said, 'How 'bout Coosie?'

'Coosie? Damn it to hell, I'd forgotten 'bout him!' His face seemed to shine with a sudden energy. 'There was a time he was courting her, long before Brecker arrived. Iffen I recall rightly it was just after her old man had been killed and they were good friends then. I couldn't imagine the old-timer with such a young woman, could you?'

'Not really but you never know.'

A silence fell over us as we both thought about Dyer, Coosie, Brecker and Raley; trying to piece the whole story together.

Finally I thought out aloud, 'That doesn't explain Raley and Brecker, does it?'

Hardtack reached out for the bottle and I gave it up. He took a shallow swig and said, 'What if Coosie was thinking that if Brecker and Chrissie ever did get married, she'd come out to the ranch, and he'd have to live under the same roof as her...'

'And he couldn't stomach that, so he told Raley 'bout the cows.'

Hardtack nodded. 'Makes sense.'

I held up a hand. 'Wait a minute! We're accusin' a dead man here. He ain't around to defend hisself and besides we got no real proof that he did all that.'

Hardtack slumped back with a look of defeat. 'Well, that's no help at all,' he was saying, waving the bottle of bourbon in the air. 'How are we supposed to get to the bottom of this?'

'You tell me,' I said defeatedly.

'Tell me what?' Maureen said, as she entered the room. Neither of us had heard the door open and were taken by surprise. 'And who said you could give Hardtack anything to drink? Are you trying to kill him?'

Hardtack waved her away. 'I'm dead anyhows. So it don't matter none.'

No doubt she'd heard it all before from dying men, women and children. But she wasn't one who was likely to let them leave this world that easily. She wagged her finger at the Texan. 'Now you listen to me, young man. We'll have no more talking about dying, d'you hear me? And if Cal is to stay any longer you'll have to give me that bottle.' She held out her hand like a school ma'am.

There was a look of defiance in Hardtack's eyes. Lifting the bottle to his lips he drained whatever was left, then handed it over with a playful smile.

'Texans!' she said.

And Hardtack came back with, 'Long may they live!'

We all laughed at that. But the laughter was hollow as each of us in that room knew that Hardtack was right. He was going to die. It was just that no one knew how long he was going to hold on to life for.

Maureen seemed to know that me and Hardtack wanted to be alone, so she left us.

I said, 'There are some things that ought to be sorted out, Hardtack. Like who's your next of kin? An' what you want done with your gear? You made out a will?'

'Hey, Cal! Quit actin' like a mother hen, it don't suit you none.' He sighed heavily and rolled over to his side and reached down the side of the bed. He brought up a sheaf of paper and handed it to me. 'There you go, boss. All legal and correct. The doc was a witness to my mark, so don't let no one say otherwise.'

I held the paper without reading it and put it down on the bedside table. 'I'll take care of that later, Hardtack. But let me an' you try an' sort this affair out. Now who have we got?'

Together we came up with a short-list of those who would benefit from the Leaning B going belly-up. It was a very short list. Dave Raley headed it, followed by Christine Dyer only because she would get money back from any land sale. By that token Hardtack said my name should be on that list; so I added it to it.

By this time Hardtack looked tired. There was still the news about the headless vet to tell him, so I made myself busy in Maureen's kitchen and brewed up some fresh coffee.

When I got back Hardtack was dead. I sat down on the edge of the bed and felt a sudden emptiness in my stomach. This part of Montana was filled with death and I was feeling sick about being around so much of it.

I stared around the room as though waiting for Hardtack to wake from sleeping. Obviously he wouldn't, and for once in my life I felt helpless. From what had started out as a simple bodyguard job to a young rancher, it had now changed beyond any of my experiences. Somewhere, out there, there was someone who wanted the Leaning B so badly they would stop at nothing.

I went into the surgery and leant against the door frame for support. Maureen turned around and looked at me. She put a hand to her mouth. She knew without me having to speak that the Texan had died. Of course she must have seen my kind of look on many faces but death still managed to surprise her.

'He knew he was dying,' she said in a weak whisper. 'He told me this afternoon.'

'I'm glad that you didn't take his leg off, Maureen.'

'Sure,' she said.

'No, I mean it. He died with some kind of grace. You've read dime novels where the hero dies with his boots on? Well, that's what Hardtack would've wanted. Boots on, and body whole.'

She took off her spectacles and cleaned them on her apron, just to do something with her hands. 'I … we did agree on that, Cal. To leave him be. That was the very least we could do for him'

I nodded. 'But you know the damnedest thing, Maureen? I ain't no nearer finding out who did that to him.' My hand crept closer to my pistol, seeking comfort in its grips. 'Everything's still so cloudy I just want to go out and get Raley.'

'You sure that it is Raley behind all this?' she asked.

I looked about the room, trying to find help for an answer.

'Everything seems so obvious. He took the cattle from Brecker; his land lies adjacent to the Leaning B and if he got a hold of it he could double his spread. Why else did he want a showdown with Brecker? If he got the kid to draw he'd've shot him down and taken the land, anyhows.'

'But you were there.'

'Yeah, for what it was worth.'

'Don't think so little of yourself, Cal. You're just frustrated now, but you'll win through in the end.'

'Seems that Raley got what he wanted, though. Brecker dead, and the cattle.'

There was a quiet rage building up inside of me. I only had to think about Coosie, Hardtack, Brecker, the old frontier cavalryman and even Weatherly. All dead. And for what? The only motive behind all those deaths was greed. One man's greed to possess something that wasn't rightly his. Whoever it was didn't deserve a chance. Or only as much as he gave the others.

Maureen could have been guessing what I was thinking when she said, 'You're going to face down Raley, aren't you?'

I could see that she was frightened. My feelings towards her had grown deeper over the last few weeks. But, Christ Almighty, there was someone out there killing people whom I called friends.

The time for tippytoeing around was finished.

What I had to do was a duty to those I had said I would help. I had given them my word; as Hardtack reminded me not so long ago, if I couldn't keep that, then what else was there left for me?

NINE

Christine Dyer also had the right to know what was going on. I left Maureen alone in the surgery, the sadness in her face still imprinted in my mind's eye, determined to get this affair over with. The light was bleeding out of the day and a gash of crimson crossed the skyline. Along the sidewalks some lamps had been lit and their light flickered dimly in the evening gloom.

Across the street Dyer's store was lit up brightly but the noise of shouting betrayed the gentleness of the scene. As I neared it the voices grew louder and more distinct. I instantly recognised Johnny Evans's voice and that of Christine's but the other was unknown to me. I had almost made it to the sidewalk when the shop door banged open and Evans's frame filled the doorway.

He was backing slowly out of the shop, his face set in grim determination. The scattergun was pointed in front of him, both hammers fully cocked. My hand dropped immediately to my handgun and rested there.

'You ain't gonna shoot no one. You hear me?' Evans was saying, his voice low and growling.

'T'ain't nothin' to lose, lawman,' came the reply from the unknown man still inside.

Evans *was* a lawman, there was no way he could hide it. He wasn't one of those who would let his deputies do the dirty work for him. He loved his job, had a pride in it, and enjoyed letting other people see this. Right now, he was enjoying this encounter. He said, 'Just lower the rifle and come on in quietly.'

The other man laughed. 'You blast me with that Greener and you'll hit the lady as well. Why don't you back off? Me and her have got some unfinished business.'

I could hear the drink in the man's voice

but there was some steel in there as well. I tried to picture what the man was up to. Obviously he was very near Christine, or even had her in front of him and it seemed that if John did let loose with the shotgun she might get hurt.

I stepped back into the shadows and moved round to the rear of the store. I remembered that there was a back door to the store; found it and slowly opened it. This door led on to a darkened passageway which in turn led to the main parlour, from there another door opened out into the main store itself. I drew out the pistol and hauled back on the hammer, then as quietly as I could began to make my way through the parlour.

Evans was keeping the man talking, their voices deadened by the closed door. As long as they kept up their talking, then neither would think about pulling the trigger. I stopped outside the parlour door, the one that led itself into the main store, and listened.

Evans was saying, '…not to blame. You've

cut your wolf loose and you don't know what you're saying.'

'I can hold my drink better than any man alive I know! So don't be givin' me a sermon on drinkin', lawdog!'

'Come on,' Christine joined in, 'let's be reasonable about this. What's this all about, anyway? A few dollars owing to you and your partner, that's all.'

'Me an' Josh is owed nigh on a hunnert dollars apiece. An' I want payin'!'

'Like I told your confederate, you'll both be paid when the job is completed.' There was a smugness in Christine's voice which made my skin crawl.

'You satisfied now, Jeb?' Evans asked. 'You gonna put the rifle down and come with me?'

'You arrestin' me, Marshal?'

'Nah, we just gonna take a pass over to my place and have us a couple of cups of Arbuckle's and forget this whole thing ever took place.'

'That all?' The drunk sounded unsure.

'Yeah, I'm sure. That right, Mrs Dyer, you won't be bringing charges against Jeb here, will you?'

Christine said in her nice-as-pie voice, 'Oh, no. Nothing of the kind. There was no harm done. Just a little discord, shall we call it?'

'If you're sure,' the drunk said.

'Sure I'm sure,' Evans replied.

You could hear the hammer being eased off by the drunk and his spurs jangled on the wooden floorboards.

'That's right, Jeb. Give me that old rifle and we'll go, yeah? That's better ... now we'll both go on over to my office and have that coffee... Sorry that he bothered you, ma'am.'

'No, no bother, really.'

I had my hand on the door knob, ready to go into the store when Christine shouted, 'Look out!'

The sound of the handgun was deafening in the small passageway. I flung the door open wide and ran into the room with my Colt out in front of me. I froze for a second or two looking at the pistol in Christine's single-handed grip. Smoke curled lazily out of the barrel. She looked around at me, and for one crazy minute I thought she was going to shoot me. 'He had a gun. He was going to kill the marshal.'

I rushed into the room, ran past her, then out of the store into the street. Evans was standing holding his scattergun and a rifle. He seemed to be in shock. A few feet away from him there was a man sprawled on his back. His mouth was opened wide as were his sightless eyes. There was a lot of blood soaking through his grey cotton shirt, spreading wider by the second. It was a killing shot. She'd either been damned lucky or it was a good shot. I stood there for a moment, trying to think. A small crowd had began to gather gawping at the dead man, and looking on in utter amazement at Christine Dyer. Standing in the store doorway she returned their looks impassively. The gun was still in her hand, but down at her side.

I looked up at her and saw that same

stony-faced look she wore when we first found out we were going to be co-partners in the Leaning B. Slowly, as if sensing me looking at her, she turned her head slightly to face me but there was no expression on her face. Then Evans snapped out of his scare and began to order people away. I bent down and closed the dead man's eyelids.

John Evans came over to me and said, 'All right, Cal. I'll deal with this from here.' He looked down at the dead man and then up at Christine saying, ''Fraid you're gonna have to come with me, ma'am.'

'I … he was going to shoot you.'

Evans shook his head. 'He weren't armed, ma'am.'

'But … his hand … he had a gun…'

Evans pushed the man's rifle in my hand and bent down to pick up the silver harmonica which the man dropped. He held it up for her to see it more clearly. 'Jeb loved to play this, ma'am. This is what he had in his hand, not a gun.'

'But … but…'

'Lock up the shop and come with me, please.'

Christine seemed a beaten woman. Her shoulders sagged, and without a further word, handed Evans the pistol she had just used to kill with. I watched as she shut the shop, and when they came level with me, Evans asked for the rifle back. I hesitated for a moment because it was only then that I looked at it for the first time. It was a Burnside Spencer carbine, just like the one the old ex-frontier cavalryman owned.

Evans held out his hand and I gave him the rifle without a comment. In return he gave me a peculiar look before speaking to one of his deputies who had arrived, nodding over to the dead body. The younger lawman nodded solemnly and went off in the other direction, probably to find the undertaker.

Not once did it occur to either Christine or Evans to ask why I was there. Or how I came to be running out of the back of the store. Or even of how much I had overheard. Tucking both the scattergun and the carbine under one arm, Evans took Christine by the arm and they walked across the street like two lovers, arm in arm, down to his office then slammed the door shut behind them.

The crowd seemed to reappear as if by magic and the editor of the local newspaper was busy interviewing people. There was also a photographer setting up his cumbersome plate camera and flash tray, trying to get the best angle for his photograph. I stood there with a hundred thoughts rushing through my head, when Doc Bay interrupted them by asking me what had happened. When I finished telling her she said, 'She'll be out by morning, just you see.'

'What makes you think that?'

She smiled. 'You don't think that Christine's lawyer will let her stand trial for murder, do you?'

I didn't know what to think.

'No, she'll be out and if she ever gets to court she'll be let off. They'll say it was an accident – she was defending the marshal whom she thought was going to be shot. A case of misadventure.'

'You sound like you've heard it all before.'

'I have.'

I couldn't keep the surprise out of my voice. 'What?'

'Didn't you know that before she came to Huntings, Christine Dyer had to leave Wyoming for killing a man?'

Well, that was news to me.

'She killed a man for attacking her in a familiar way, if you know what I mean.'

I nodded yes. 'Did he get it in the heart as well?'

'Yes. As well as the lower region.'

I couldn't help but smile. 'I thought it was too good a shot.'

The doc linked her arm in mine and steered me away from the scene. 'What about tonight? Are you still going to see Raley?' The worry was back in her voice.

'I've got to.'

She sighed. 'I see. Then perhaps you ought to know that he is in town right now having a meeting with some business people over at the Kemble Palace Hotel.'

I stopped abruptly and demanded, 'You've known this all along?'

'No, I overheard it from a DR rider I was treating for busted bones and cuts a moment ago. He reckons that the Leaning B have been cutting DR fences and letting the cattle wander away.'

'Done what?'

'I'm only repeating what this cowboy told me.' She clung tighter to my arm. 'Cal, I'm really worried. I don't want anything to happen to you. This cowboy also said that Raley's mad. Mad enough to start a full blown range war.'

Through her glasses I could see the fear dancing in her eyes. That was the last thought on my mind; a range war where no one wins.

'War? Did I hear someone say war?'

Jake Latchford seemed to appear out of thin air. He was dressed in his finest Sunday-go-to-meeting clothes but his long face seemed at odds with them. 'So what's this

217

you're sayin' Doc?'

She still had her arm linked in mine, holding on to it a little tighter, stopping me pulling away. She looked up at me and waited for me to explain. I had to start by telling him about Hardtack's death, and finished off with Christine Dyer's shooting of old Jeb. What I didn't tell him was the latest bit of news that the doc told me about the woman. I didn't think it had anything to do with our troubles at the Leaning B.

'So what war you talkin' about?' asked Jake again.

'Seems that Raley's been accusin' us of cutting his bob wire and letting his cattle roam,' I said.

'He ain't the one who should go around pointin' the finger.'

I said, 'Meanin'?'

The ramrod straightened back his shoulders, standing square. 'Meanin' that since you've been away from the ranch a whole bunch of DR rannies rode in an' scattered the remuda to the four winds. We ain't got but six cow ponies between us now.'

I drew in a deep breath and held it for a moment before letting it go. 'Jake, you got the others with you?'

'Nope, only Lowman, Swede, Mills and myself are left now.'

'Christ! What's happened to the others?'

'Gone to Texas. Who knows? They were tired of being threatened by the law and Raley.'

I nodded my head slowly understanding their feelings. 'Well, seems as if I get to see Raley on my own,' I said.

'You've got me to help you, Cal,' said Jake.

'No. This is something I've got to do by myself. No sense in getting anyone else killed if I can help it.'

Maureen released her arm and kissed me lightly on the lips. She whispered, 'Be careful, Cal.'

I tried a reassuring smile but I don't think it came out that way. I turned to Jake and said, 'Do me a favour, Jake? Take care of the doc for me? If she tries something stupid …

don't know what but keep her at the surgery anyhows.'

'Why don't you take one of the boys with you to watch your back?' Jake insisted.

'OK, then. If Lowman is in town I'll take him. I think I need a man with a good eye.'

'Yeh, over at the stables taking care of the ponies.'

'OK, I'll fetch him.' I began to walk away, saying over my shoulder, 'Remember what I said. Keep her safe for me.'

'Trust me, Cal,' Jake called after me. 'Trust me.'

From where the stable stood the Kemble Palace Hotel was the largest building that could be seen. Three storeys high, built of red brick and planks with painted white trim. The streets were packed with men, women, children, buggies, wagons and riders heading for the circus. Fireworks cracked and banged; lighting up the night air.

As Lowman and me walked shoulder to shoulder down the street I kept my eye on a man standing by the hitching rail outside the Kemble. He was heavily armed: he wore a double rig, a shoulder holster showing on the outside and carried a long-barrelled Winchester. I looked around for more men like him. Whether they were hidden in the shadows or inside the Kemble I didn't know. Perhaps he was a man who worked alone. That may be so, but the questions was 'who for?' And was he ready to die for his employer? Johnny Lowman must have spotted him just then; he gave me a nudge in the ribs.

'I see him,' I said.

'D'you know him?'

Even with the light from the hotel windows and doorway I didn't recognise him. 'No. You?'

Lowman gave it a thought. 'He ain't from around here. His clothes say he's from down south.'

We carried on walking. We were only twenty feet away when he noticed us. He pushed himself away from the upright, blocking our way into the Kemble. We carried on. He stood there, body tensed, muscles bunched – waiting. Lowman was at my shoulder breathing heavy. Maybe scared, maybe not. This was one time he had to be strong.

'You can't go in,' the gunman said.

'Come on, boy. Move out of the way,' I said.

He wiped his hand on the leg of his jeans, leaving it near his pistol.

'There's a private party goin' on inside, an' you can't go in without an invitation,' he stated.

'Don't be stupid, son,' Lowman said. 'We've come to see Raley.'

'Who are you?'

'We're friends,' I lied. 'Probably he forgot to put us on the list.'

'No shit?'

'Hey, boy! You got any idea who you're talking to?' Lowman demanded.

Gunman looked at me, then at Lowman. He looked back at me. He half smiled and said, 'A couple of saddle-bums is all I see.'

I heard Lowman move just before he punched the gunman in the face. His head was rocked back and a blob of blood flecked the sidewalk. Lowman whacked him again, and the gunman dropped the Winchester and went down on one knee.

'You're a dead man!' he snarled.

Then the bastard went for his shoulder gun.

I pulled my gun first and shot him in the face. Lowman jumped out of the way of the splattering blood and gore.

'Shit! Shit! You didn't have to kill him, Cal!'

'Maybe not, but I wasn't going to wait around to find out if he was prepared to shoot either of us. So much for him,' I said.

I stepped over the body and went into the Kemble. Inside the lobby a couple of suited men looked around at me as the batwings doors flapped shut. A man and a woman standing at the registration desk were open-mouthed in fear. They moved out of the way as I walked over to the counter, the gun still in my hand.

'Can I help you, sir?' asked the clerk as calm as anyone could be in this situation.

'Where's Raley?'

'I don't know, sir,' he said. His large Adam's apple bobbed up and down. 'He and his party left the hotel a half hour ago.'

'Where'd they go?'

'I have no idea, sir.'

'Then you don't mind me looking around?'

I circled the lobby, ignoring the looks I was getting. I entered the dining-room, pacing slowly through the half-empty room taking a good look at the diners. There was no one there I recognised. I went out of the opposite door and took the stairs to the first floor. I ignored the bedrooms, looking for the bigger state rooms. I came to the end of the hall, turned and went down the other corridor.

Half-way down two men were leaning against the wall. One was picking his nose and the other scratching his head. They saw me, saw the gun in my hand and pushed themselves away.

I raised the gun, saying, 'Don't! Don't do anything. Keep your hands away from them irons.' My voice was hard and the men responded to the menace in it.

Nose-picker said, 'Wait! Wait!' He pushed his hands high into the air.

'Who the hell are you?' the other demanded.

I said nothing, keeping the gun on them.

'Jesus, mister. What d'you want?' Nose-picker said.

'Raley.'

'He ain't here,' the braver of the two said.

'So,' I said, 'You gonna tell me, or do you want me to beat it out of you?'

I watched the weaker one breathe through his nose, his shifting eyes on mine. He was trying to decide.

Finally, 'The circus.'

'What?'

'He's gone to the circus with the others. Ringside seats, you can bet on that.'

I nodded. 'I shot the man out front. Don't

make me shoot you as well. You want me to do the same thing, shoot your face off, then come after me an' I'll oblige.'

The clerk looked up as I came thumping down the stairs, a frightened smile plastered on his face. He stepped away from the counter like it had suddenly become red hot, bumping into a captain's chair. Johnny Lowman stood inside the lobby, his face turned out to the street. There was no one else in the lobby. He looked around and stared at me for a moment. His eyes were slightly glazed with shock. Blood was drying black on his boots and on the cuffs of his jeans.

'You're right,' I said to the clerk. 'Raley ain't here.' Then walked past the desk slowly, knowing that the clerk was watching me, nervous of me. I stepped up to Lowman and said, 'You're gonna have to leave the rest to me, Johnny.'

He cocked his head to one side and asked, 'Why?'

'I don't want to see you killed.'

'Who's gonna kill me?'

'Well, for a start he would have done.' I jerked my head to the dead gunman on the other side of the batwings. 'He was a paid killer, and I figger that he ain't the only one in town. I'll take any more chances on my own. I don't want you killed; there's been enough death on the Leaning B. And tonight will see the end of it – one way or the other.'

'You're asking me to walk away, is that it?'

'Yeah.'

The cowboy looked down at his boots, then back at me. 'We should do this together, Cal.'

I shook my head. 'I don't need your help. I'm gonna handle Raley my way. But thanks for your assistance.'

Johnny Lowman walked out of the hotel without looking back.

After a couple of heartbeats I followed in his wake. Outside I drew in a long gulp of air, held it for a second or two, then blew it out. The gunman lay on the floor untouched, unattended. The final outflow of blood oozed across the wooden walkway before soaking into the planking.

TEN

Somewhere down the street came shouting that had nothing to do with celebrating the circus's arrival. I knew it wouldn't be too long before someone reported the fact that there was a dead man lying on the walkway outside the Kemble. I looked at the gunman's face and slowly shook my head, then stepped off the sidewalk into the street.

I turned into Main Street and found it very crowded. Old and young mingled together, and I pushed my way into the mainstream of people. There was an avenue of torches lighting our way to the circus's main entrance. The pace slowed as we grew nearer. The children were excited, and their joy seemed to infect the parents and others. They smiled and swapped pleasantries to whoever shuffled along next to them.

The big top tent was massive. Its multi-coloured canvas seemed to glow in the dark as it loomed high into the air. Above the human noises the animals were making their presence known. Tigers roared, horses neighed and a strange trumpeting overrode all these. It was hard not to feel any excitement but I had to control it, fight it down, and concentrate on what I had come for.

As we neared the big top there were three deputies standing by the pay kiosk. They were taking weapons from whoever showed them. There was no way I was going to hand over my revolver so I drew it and hid it down the back of my trousers, covering it with my shirt and vest. I paid the 25¢ and went inside.

Most of the inside had been taken up with seats that rose up in tiers, all surrounding a large sawdust ring. Many of the seats were already taken, especially the front rows which the children had claimed. The folks behind me didn't give me time to scan the crowds; they pushed me on fighting to get seats of their own. I went with the flow of the crowd; searching through the mass of faces as we went. It wasn't an easy task finding Raley among the people but I guessed that if he was with businessmen he would be out to impress them. What better way was there than to have the best seats in the house?

I spotted him about four rows back in a cordoned-off section. He sat with three other men all dressed city-style; all smiles, laughter and sucking on a big cigar. There seemed to be only one way to reach the area and that was to go most of the way around the ring. I pushed myself between the canvas and the seats as they began to rise in the air. I pulled out my revolver and pushed it into the holster, then began to make my way around the back of the seats.

The noise from the crowd died down to a hush. From where I was I couldn't see why. Then a voice, loud and clear, suddenly announced, 'Ladies and gentlemen. Boys and girls. Tonight is no ordinary night.

Tonight you will be thrilled, excited and left in wondrous amazement. You will witness feats of strength, fire-eaters, death-defying sure-shooting and a multitude of animals gathered from all over the world. Yes, ladies and gentlemen, boys and girls, welcome to Woodrow Brooke's Circus World!'

His announcement was met with thunderous applause and I used the noise to mask my movements in creeping around to where Raley sat. Soon I was behind the section, and the only way there was to climb up a guy line to reach the top of the seating area. I began the climb, and startled a couple of circus-goers by my sudden appearance but they began to clap, thinking I was part of the act.

To many of the audience my balancing act on the back of the seating was entertaining. I didn't want to spoil the illusion, so I used this to my advantage and made my way down to the enclosure.

When I reached the section the men were talking business.

'Why, yes, we'll help you. We've said that all along.' The speaker was moustachioed, its ends waxed to fine points and he spoke with a strangled accent.

'Och, man, you'll no go starvin'!' This man's accent was even stranger. 'There'll be plenty o' money. All cash.'

Raley didn't turn his head.

'I ain't worried,' he said. 'I know you gents will ante up for them cows.'

'What seems to be the problem?' moustache said.

'I'll tell you the problem,' I said.

On hearing my voice, all four of them jerked involuntarily.

'Calhoun!' Raley spluttered.

'Who?' asked one of the men.

I pulled out the revolver and pressed it into the soft flesh of Raley's flabby jowls. His eyes bulged in their sockets and flinched when I hauled back on the hammer.

'See here, sir! I don't...'

'Shut up!' I ordered.

'Well, I never...'

'An' you never will,' said his fellow busi-
nessman with a good Yankee accent. 'If you
don't keep that mouth of yourn shut!'

I thanked him for taking the words out of
my mouth.

Raley said, 'What d'you want, Calhoun?'

'Seems to me, Raley, that you were about
to cut a deal with these gents.'

'Yeah, an'?'

'An', if I ain't mistaken, you was going to
sell them Leaning B property.'

The three businessmen exchanged puzzled
looks. Moustache said, 'Mister Calhoun,
may I introduce myself? I am Laurence
Cooper from London, England. This gentle-
man is David McPherson and this is Mister
James Osborne of the Cattlemen's Asso-
ciation. Do I understand you correctly in
that you are suggesting Mister Raley is
knowingly selling stolen cattle?'

'Yep.'

'And what, may I ask, do you intend to do
with that pistol? Blow his head off?'

'Mayhaps.'

He wagged a finger under my nose. 'Not a very astute piece of thinking. You may not be able to see them but I assure you sir, there are more hired gunmen here than your gun contains bullets. Should you succeed in killing Mister Raley you would certainly forfeit your own life. And to what avail? We must be able to conclude this matter amiably, must we not?' Cooper spoke in a calm assured manner.

After the initial shock Cooper simply began to take command of the situation. I had to hand it to the Englishman, he was calm. But he wasn't that calm.

'Listen, Mister Cooper,' I said, 'my argument is with Raley. I don't want to spray his blood and brains all over your nice suits. If you doubt that I couldn't kill you and the other two before your gunnies came for me – think again.'

I moved the gun away from Raley's face but kept it out of reach from Cooper whose face had blanched slightly. But if there was any danger here it would come from him.

I said, 'Now, Raley. What I want you to do is get up nice 'n' easy like and walk out of here. We've got business of our own to sort out.'

Cooper began to rise out of the chair. I pushed him back down saying, 'That invitation doesn't stretch to you, friend.'

'Now wait a minute!' Cooper exclaimed, rising out of the chair again.

I laid the barrel off the revolver alongside his head and Cooper slumped back down. Osborne and McPherson paled but sat still.

'Gentlemen,' I said, 'your deal is off. You make a move after us and I'll use the right end of this revolver to stop you. Understand?'

They nodded yes.

I lowered the revolver and pushed it hard against Raley's rib. 'Move out,' I told him. 'Try anythin' an' I'll blow your heart out of your ribs!'

I pushed Raley in the small of the back, keeping him out in front, and my gun out of reach.

'You really think you're gonna get away

with this?' Raley asked over his shoulder.

'Get away with what?'

'With whatever you've got in mind.'

'This is it, Raley. This is where it ends.'

He tried to stop but I shoved him forward, through the canvas flap and we stepped out into the night. There were a handful of circus people milling around but none of them paid us any attention, they were much too busy with their own affairs.

'Keep goin',' I said and waited until he was about six feet from me next to a gaily painted wagon box. 'Now turn around.'

'You're not gonna shoot me in the back?' he sneered.

I ignored him. 'Turn around.'

He turned to face me. 'Well?'

'Another one of our crew is dead,' I stated.

He shrugged. 'What's that got to do with me?'

'You had him killed.'

He snorted a laugh.

'Him and the cook, both. You've even tried to kill me a couple o' times.'

'You accusin' me of murder?'

'You denyin' it?'

'Do you have any idea how stupid you sound?' He relaxed a little, leaning back against one of the wagon wheels. 'What reason would I have in killing a cook, a cowboy and a drifter?'

'That's what I want to know.'

'You're scaring the hell out of me, son. I thought our argument was over a couple of cows.'

'That's how it started. Seems you've gotten greedy and want everythin'.'

'I don't know what it is about you, Calhoun, but your line of thinkin' is way off.'

I shifted a little uneasily. 'You sayin' you wouldn't have anythin' to gain by havin' Brecker's cattle and his land?'

Raley turned aggressive, ignoring my question. 'And I suppose you had nothin' to do with cuttin' our fences and poisonin' our water?'

'What?'

'Well now,' Raley said in good humour. He

looked at me with a crooked smile on his face. 'The boot's on the other foot now, ain't it?'

'Just a minute, Raley,' I said. 'Where are you headed?'

'The answer's the same when you think about it. Both the Leaning B and the DR have suffered over the last month or so. You look at the bigger picture and everythin' becomes clearer.'

We stood in the shadows watching one another. Waiting as we decided on who should be believed. This was the second time I had heard about Raley's fences being cut, though the first about poisoned water. Raley seemed to be casual, showing me that he didn't really hold a grudge. And that worried me. Surely he knew that our paths were going to cross and more than likely we were going to fight? But now I was unsure of him, of the whole situation. Had someone been trying to play us off against each other, waiting to see the results? No doubt they had hoped that either one of us would be dead by now. That would have solved their problem for them.

'You ain't authorised to carry a gun here, Calhoun.' Evans's voice sounded loud behind me.

'John,' I said without turning around.

'Sounds like you expected me.'

'Nothing about you would surprise me.'

'Well, Cal,' Evans laughed easily, 'you know me.'

'Sure do, you sonofabitch!'

The jingle-jangle of his spurs announced his approach and my muscles bunched up ready for his attack. But he surprised me once again by doing nothing. Instead, he came up alongside me and said, 'Hand over your gun, Cal.'

'No.'

'No?'

'No.'

Evans sighed. 'You don't seem to understand the situation here, do you?'

'That's all he don't understand,' Raley added.

'I didn't want this kind of trouble,' Evans was saying as he walked around to face me but keeping out of Raley's way. 'I hoped you would have got the message and ridden on. But no, not big man Calhoun, you just had to stick around and mess things up.'

'Let's settle this now, John,' I said. 'We'll fight. Fist fight, gun fight, you name it. I ain't waiting around any longer.'

The town marshal chuckled. 'Me? Fist fight you? Why you must be a touched addled up top.' His tone shifted to a hard-edged one. 'I'll settle it right now by putting a bullet between your eyes!' he snarled.

'Where do you come in all this, John? Raley I can understand but you? What do you gain from it?'

'Hell, I told you I was on my way out as the lawman here. What have I got left? I began investing money in buying shares in cattle. Something went badly wrong with a drive in Arizona. The herd was all but lost, but my money all went south.'

'Your money or the taxes?' I sneered.

'Right.'

'And what better way of getting it back but by helping to steal Brecker's cattle and sell them on to Raley?'

'Now the boy uses his brains,' Raley said.

'The Leaning B is finished,' said Evans. 'Most of your men have been scared off. The remuda's depleted and at this moment the herd has been scattered across the range.'

'Money. That's all you were in this for, John?' I asked.

'The only kind I know is what you can hold in your hands,' he replied, speaking like he was right and nothing else mattered.

Raley brought out a cigar and lit up. 'Brecker would have run the Leaning B into the ground sooner or later. His death kind of speeded things up. You should have walked away while you could.'

I leapt across the space between myself and Evans. I brushed aside his gunhand, and butted the lawman in the face. He staggered back and I chopped down on his wrist with my pistol. There was a satisfying crack, and Evans cried out. I stepped inside his flailing outstretched arm and threw a punch that broke his nose and jarred my wrist right up to the elbow. Evans fell down heavily on his back.

'I want you alive,' I said softly. But to make sure he was out of it I stomped on his head with my boot heel.

The time to finally settle the score with Raley had come. No more talking, no more accusations; this was it. Satisfied that I was doing something at last I turned to face him but he had gone. A sharp pang of disappointment struck my chest and I cursed aloud and ran over to the wagon.

The circus people had arranged their wagons in arrow-straight lines; leaving small alleyways between them. Looking down the line I caught a glimpse of Raley ducking off to the right. Gingerly, with the gun out in front, I went after him.

Away to my right the mighty roar of a grizzly bear shattered the night air. I ran that way. Within seconds I reached the wagon where the grizzly was a caged prisoner. The bear was frantically pacing up and down. Its massive yellow teeth showed in its mouth as great globules of saliva dripped down. But there was no sign of Raley. I searched around the cage but he wasn't hiding around there. Obviously he had passed this way, circus people would be familiar to the bear and only a stranger would cause its agitation. I went down on my knees and checked under the wagons. About fifteen feet away I saw someone showing a clean pair of bootheels heading back towards the circus big top. The sneaky sonofa was doubling back.

I raced back, retracing my steps but didn't reach Evans in time to stop Raley picking up the town marshal's Colt.

'Raley!' I bellowed.

He froze for an instant but then continued to straighten up. The Colt was aimed at me, and Raley wore a crazy lop-sided grin. 'Too bad, Calhoun,' he said raising the Colt.

'Leave it be!'

Raley held the pistol out but turned to see the speaker.

'Drop it, Raley!' Lowman ordered. He was holding his own gun on Raley, his hand rock steady and face composed. He walked away from the big top canvas, eyes fixed steadily on the rancher.

Raley looked from him to me, then back again. His shoulders slumped slightly and he started to lower the Colt. But instead of giving it up he spun on his heels and fired off a shot. Lowman's thigh exploded under the bullet's impact and he crashed face down into the dirt.

I fired my gun in gut reaction but missed. Raley crouched down to make himself a smaller target. His Colt flashed and I felt the sting of the bullet slicing across my face. I let a bullet fly. It hit Raley, knocking him backwards and I heard a voice say, 'That's for Coosie.'

I took aim again and fired. I hit Raley as he was rolling himself under a wagon. All around us the caged animals were roaring, squawking and rattling their bars. Angry human voices were added to the confusion but no one came near us. I ran around the wagon as the injured rancher was hauling himself upright. He was groaning loudly with the effort and it was clear that my shots must have hit a vital spot. He slowly raised his head as I approached.

His eyes held a mixture of pain and madness. There was no sign whatsoever of fear. His crooked lop-sided grin was back on his face and he spat out some blood. I raised my pistol for the killing shot but held off. Using one blood-slicked hand on a cage bar Raley pulled himself up. I had to admit that he had a great inner strength. Then he began to raise his pistol.

Suddenly there was a flash of orange and black and Raley began to scream, screaming in a high-pitched girlish way and filled with fear that made my blood run cold. I froze to the spot with my pistol still pointing at the rancher. The cheeks of his face turned into rivers of blood. A great paw clamped down on his head and held it against the bars whilst other claws repeatedly ripped ribbons of flesh from his face and neck. I stood there shocked by the sight of the tiger ripping my enemy apart, cheating me of any revenge and I slowly, reluctantly lowered the pistol to my side.

The smell of blood seemed to excite the tiger so much that he continued raking his claws across Raley's neck and face long after the rancher had died. His body only stayed upright because the tiger had him trapped against the bars. I wasn't aware of the man standing next to me until he spoke.

'Simbah! Oh, my poor Simbah.'

I slowly turned to face him. His thin face was almost as red as his frock coat and the beady black eyes peered angrily into mine.

'If you've hurt her,' the ring master said. 'I'll have you arrested! I'll take you to court. I'll ... I'll...'

'Why don't you shut up!' I shouldered the ring master out of the way and went to see how Lowman was.

He had gotten himself into a half-sitting position with both hands pressed down across the bullet wound. Blood seeped through his fingers and stained the ground around him black. I pulled off my neckerchief and tied it above the entry wound.

'Thanks, John.'

'Uh? You didn't think you were going to have all the excitement to yourself, did you?'

I removed his neckerchief, told him to move his hands away, and pressed it over the neat hole, then told him to put the pressure back on it. By this time a lot of bystanders had gathered around, mainly circus people but there were some townsfolk among them.

Someone had brought a couple of lanterns along and taking one I went to where Evans lay on the ground. There was nothing I could do for Raley – he was way beyond help.

Looking down at the lawman's battered face I felt a deep pang of regret. What if I had killed him? I'd surely end up in jail and would lose everything I had been fighting for over the last couple of months. Dropping down to one knee I felt for a heartbeat. I panicked at first because I couldn't find it but I tried again. A minute or so later I saw his chest rise shallowly, and I breathed a sigh of relief.

'Is he still alive, Cal?'

Maureen's voice was as soft as a trickling stream to my ears. I looked up. 'Yes, but only just.'

'Here, let me take over.' She crouched down and began to work, automatically becoming the efficient doctor. 'Are you going to tell me what happened?' she asked.

So I explained everything to her. When she had finished she stood up putting a hand to my cheek. 'Cal, whatever happens,' she said. 'I'll always be here for you.'

'Thanks.' It may have only been one word but that was all I was capable of. She smiled reassuringly, and leant forward and planted a kiss on my mouth. A kiss so sweet and fleeting I could have dreamt it.

'Excuse me for buttin' in, ma'am.' It was Johnny Lowman speaking up. 'But when you've done with either patient, I need a bit of attention, too.'

Maureen laughed. 'Of course you do, cowboy. Of course you do.'

We were sitting in Maureen's front parlour. Johnny Lowman's leg was heavily bandaged, and he sat on a comfy chair near the fire drinking French brandy. Maureen was pouring the drinks at a small bureau whilst Jake Latchford leant against the mantelpiece sucking on a large cigar.

The doc handed me my drink, saying, 'I know you said that Raley and Evans were in this together but what I don't understand is how Christine Dyer was involved.'

'Well, she wasn't really involved,' I said. 'Evans was trying to set her up to make it look like she was.'

'How d'you work that out?' Latchford asked.

I started by telling them of the ex-frontier

cavalryman I'd killed and left in the mountains – the first time I'd admitted this to anyone other than Hardtack. About the Burnside carbine I'd kept and when I saw the same make carried by the man she had killed, everything seemed to fall into place.

'But why wasn't it her?' Lowman seemed disappointed.

I sighed aloud. 'Look, John, as much as I hate the woman, you didn't see the look on her face when she realised that the old boy was only reaching for his harmonica and not a gun.'

'That's it?' Jake Latchford said.

'No. The more I think of it the more it seemed like Evans was pushing me to hate her. You see, I've known Johnny Evans for some years and he was the last person I would have guessed to be working alongside Dave Raley. I thought that if it was any of you, then I guess I would have said Jake.'

'The hell!' Jake spluttered.

I put my hand up to pacify him. 'I know, Jake, but you seemed to be in the right places at the right time, and for a while I just thought…'

Maureen stepped in. 'I'm glad that you saw some sense, Cal.'

I nodded my agreement. 'Now we can get on with some serious ranching.'

'Hey! Wait a minute!' Johnny Lowman spoke up. 'What about them fellers with the Burnsides? What did they have to do with all of this?'

'Ah, it works out that Christine Dyer hired them to hunt cougar that Raley said were pestering the herds,' I explained. 'And Evans apparently had an outstanding warrant on the one called Jeb, he was the one shot by Dyer, and he blackmailed him and his partner into getting me out of the way – permanently.'

'Seems they were pretty useless,' Maureen said.

'They were successful in killing two people,' Lowman reminded us. And for a while those words silenced the room.

'So,' Maureen said. 'What are you going to

do, Cal?'

'Well, with Christine Dyer in jail waiting for the judge to decide what he was going to do, I went to see her lawyer and he handed me the deeds to the Leaning B.'

'He done what?' Lowman said.

'He explained that his client wanted no more to do with ranching or ranchers ever again. Town Marshal John Evans, once he recovers from his injuries, is going to be tried for accessory to murder on two counts; theft of public taxes and miscarriage of justice.'

I drained my drink and stood up. I looked at each of the faces in the room in turn. To Johnny Lowman, a cowboy who put his life on the line to save mine. To Jake Latchford, a man whose principles were equal to mine. And finally to Maureen Bay, a fine doctor of medicine and a woman who–

'Will you marry me, Maureen?' The words were out of my mouth before I knew it.

'Of course, you fool!' She threw herself into my arms and we embraced.

'Jake,' I heard Johnny Lowman say. 'I

don't know if I'd rather be shot or watch these two!'

'I agree, let's leave 'em be.'

The publishers hope that this book has given you enjoyable reading. Large Print Books are especially designed to be as easy to see and hold as possible. If you wish a complete list of our books please ask at your local library or write directly to:

Dales Large Print Books
Magna House, Long Preston,
Skipton, North Yorkshire.
BD23 4ND